THE PHONE IN THE FISHBOWL

JOSEPH HIRSCH

Black Rose Writing | Texas

ISBN: 978-1-68433-968-6
PUBLISHED BY BLACK ROSE WRITING
www.blackrosewriting.com

Printed in the United States of America
Suggested Retail Price (SRP) $18.95

The Phone in the Fishbowl is printed in Baskerville

*"We do not change. It is true we may be transformed,
but we always walk within our boundaries,
within the marked-off circle."*
— Ernst Jünger, *The Glass Bees*

THE PHONE IN THE FISHBOWL

ONE

Blake lay on the bed, sinking into the warm sheets. He watched Jenda as she stood in front of the mirror, combing wet strands of her dirty blond hair that was closer to brown after a shower.

She caught him staring at her reflection in the mirror, smiled. She kept combing while singing some earworm of a pop hit. That and the song of a bird on a branch outside their apartment window put him in a kind of foggy bliss from which he never wanted to wake. But he had to get up.

This was his favorite part of their life together, early in the morning before he went to work and Jenda headed off to school. Both of them clean, productive citizens holding down jobs, yet still with time to make love at a slow pace. And time to sit listening to music and birdsong, play with the cat and let the peace of the straight life slowly sink in. Maybe even let this blossom into something more.

"What are you thinking about?" She lifted her wet locks, exposing the fishtail of the multicolored kraken creature tattooed on her back. The monster (based on something from her sketchbook) usually remained concealed except when she combed her hair.

"I'm thinking I don't want to get up. And I'm thinking I like just watching you almost as much as I like sleeping with you."

Jenda stopped combing her hair, the brush caught on an obstinate strand. She broke through the tangle and asked, "Does it ever bother you when we're making love?"

"What?" He knew *what*, but maybe if he forced her to say it, she might let the subject drop.

"My past."

No such luck. "It's called the past for a reason," he said. "It's passed." He rolled over in the bed sticky with their drying, commingled sweat. "I have one, too."

"Not like mine."

He shrugged, even though she wasn't looking and couldn't appreciate the gesture. "I'm not a pretty girl. I didn't have that option. I stole money from my mom," he added. "Which was even worse." He finally stood up, but groaned as he did. "Plus, I've got my mugshot out there online for the entire world to see."

"We're going to get that case expunged."

"Yeah, but you can't expunge a mugshot. The internet never forgets."

Soren the green-eyed Siamese meowed, skittered from his hiding place beneath the ruffled edge of the bedspread. Blake watched him leap across the hardwood floor, plant all his paws on the linoleum and attack his catnip-laced, stuffed tropical fish. "I'm through with the needle."

"I'm just getting started." She smiled, pointed toward the plastic box filled with her phlebotomy tools.

It felt weird having needles so close. They were a trigger for him (or at least a temptation), but it would have been unreasonable (and somehow unmanly) for him to admit his weakness, his fear, to ask her to leave the box in her VW. She needed to practice sometimes. And only a fool would leave anything of value in the car in this neighborhood.

She set the hairbrush down and turned around. She examined her rear in the mirror, bounced up and down to confirm the presence or absence of fat. There was a slightly buoyant jiggle, but it was the straining of muscle overlain in a softly contoured layer of fat rather than the cottage cheese-like cellulite of a few months ago. Not that he had minded her former figure. "I need to get a tat there."

"How about a heart that says 'Mother' with an arrow through it?"

"I hate my mom," she said. "And I got to lose some weight first, before I even think about adding ink."

"No, you don't." He watched her watch her ass in the mirror, then looked her in the eye. He drank in her smile and smiled back at her.

*

Telesolutions was in a redbrick, five story building in Midtown across from a bus stop and the Hope Ways Clinic. Hope Ways was housed in a strange postmodern building shaped like an amphitheater band shell. It gave the otherwise-shabby neighborhood a futuristic touch. Sometimes while working Blake would look out the window at the clinic, marveling at how far he'd come in his recovery but how close that other world remained.

He avoided looking at the bus stop too much because it reminded him of the grim commute awaiting him before he could get home and be happy again with Jenda, when they could screw and talk away the stress of the day. He'd get a car soon. He had to. Sure, she seemed to associate the good life with bad times and wanted nothing more to do with the sugar daddies, but she deserved to have a guy who wasn't a total loser, or to have to associate sobriety with poverty.

Or not poverty…Getting by, which maybe was even worse, since it was less dramatic.

Blake picked up the phone, grateful for the distraction the job provided. His finger went down the line on the list of prospects, four previous ones (two check marks, one question mark, and one "X" where he struck out mainly because he hadn't had his morning cup of coffee when he called).

He dialed the number, let it ring, spun in his swivel chair away from the window, using his legs to brace himself between the two partitions that marked him as a good seller. He was a thoroughbred barely contained in his stall between first place showings. He stared across the expanse of grey looped carpet, toward the other side of the office, the Fishbowl, where Collections got handled (or rather didn't most of the time).

"George Washington Carver Elementary, Administrator Stevenson here. How may I help you?"

No secretary meant the man was his own buffer. Could be good or bad. But then again, no buffer meant maybe no budget. Blake kept swiveling, caught a face-full of sunshine through the window as he spun, used the toe of his right loafer to brake himself. "Mr. Stevenson."

"*Dr.* Stevenson."

A bit of a hard-ass, maybe. No problem. Working with elementary kids required it. "Dr. Stevenson." He used the preferred title but didn't apologize for going with "Mr." at the outset. "I'm calling on behalf of Top Vend Family Brands to see if you might be interested…"

"You must not read the news." The man scoffed.

Barely anyone read the news anymore. They watched it. But he held his tongue, waited. A good salesman was not merely a good talker. He listened.

"State initiative had those machines pulled from the schools. Too many kids looking like glazed hams. I've seen them with my own eyes. Getting so big even the bullies couldn't stuff them in their lockers."

Blake didn't have to fake the laugh, for which he was grateful. He hated the hard sellers, the cornballs, the oil slicks, as much as the customers did. He didn't have to run a con. The product was a good one. "I hear you, Dr. Stevenson." People usually loved to hear their names. Blake didn't want to be presumptuous, but already knew the guy liked his title. "Which is why I want you to know that Top Vend is a green vendor, and because there are no trans fats, saturated fats, no additives or high fructose corn syrup, the statewide ban does not apply to them." He thought about mentioning the revenue share with the school, but held off. He'd already given the man pause.

"That's different." Dr. Stevenson grunted, clucked his tongue, then spoke again. "Yeah, well, we still have to worry about vandalism, kids busting into the machines. Then you got kids willing to steal from their siblings or other students. It's a discipline issue. If it was just on this side of the house…"

The doctor paused. Blake took the opening, skipped the spiel about how the machines were tamper-resistant and had antitheft designs, because that wouldn't address one kid holding another upside down and snatching the quarters that fell out of his pockets. "This side of the house?"

"Administration," the administrator said. "On this side of the building. The classrooms are in another wing."

"So there are only adults on your side of the house?"

"Thank God." Another gruff laugh.

"That's perfect. Because we offer balanced meals for adults. We have a whole vending line of soups, rices, and noodle dishes…"

"Yeah, why not? My ass is here sixteen hours a day. And I need to lose some weight, set the standard for these little monsters." There was another pause from the doctor's end of the line. "Listen, send me some literature and we'll see if we can't work something out. Wouldn't hurt at least to bring it up at the next meeting."

Blake picked up his ballpoint pen, clicked it, prepared to write the address. But before that, he went back over the ledger with the list of prospects. Put a "?" next to the man's name, made an arrow that led to the margin, where he scribbled a note-to-self. "Prefers to be called doctor."

*

He was zoning, riding the back of a bronco that had thrown many a man free and left him trampled underfoot. He couldn't pretend that selling solved it all the same way heroin had, but it got the blood buzzing. He had a handful more prospects for the day, and then something Bill wanted to break his balls about. Then the plan was to duck out a little early (with Bill's okay), do some sleuthing on the Eucalady line they were getting ready to push. That way he could get ahead of the competition when they switched over from the vending contract to the moisturizing lotion line.

But his phone was ringing and blinking. An incoming call, and not a prank or some other silly crap from inside the office. It was coming from outside, and because the clinic had agreed not to call him here, that narrowed it down.

Blake picked up the phone. "Hello?"

"Bla-ake?"

"Mom, I'm at work."

"I know, but this is important."

"So's work."

"There's a letter coming to your apartment. Fill it out to the best of your knowledge if you want to stay on Mel's insurance plan."

"Okay." He shrank inside, the confidence contracting, squeezed out of him like pulp pressed from an orange. A minute ago he had been a salesman nonpareil, a symphony of motion and dexterous money-making. Now he was a twenty-something year old ex-heroin addict whose class B felony still haunted him, who only got his Suboxone because his mother's husband had mercy on him, whose mugshot was online for the world to see, hair a disheveled mess and eyes red-ringed from sleeplessness and crying his tear ducts dry.

Plus, he took the bus to work.

"I'll get it and fill it out." He kept his voice down, head so low his chin touched his sternum.

"And how's Jenna doing?"

"Jenda's good," he said, hitting the "d" in his girlfriend's name hard, hoping his mother would hear it. But if she hadn't heard it the first ten-thousand times, and her eye somehow overlooked it when she saw it written, this time would not be any different.

"I mean with your case."

"Mom, the plan was always for her to get through school, then we would both pool our resources to look into the expungement."

Then he could be free, as free as anyone could be of their past. But no way was he letting Jenda pay for the lawyer to look into his case by herself. That was all he needed, to be dependent not only on his mother, but his girlfriend. A true deadbeat burdening multiple women.

"Okay, honey. I just wanted to check in with you."

"I appreciate it. And I love you, Ma. But I got to go."

"Goodbye, dear."

He hung up before she could think of something else, exhaled hard, as if the woman who gave birth to him, a woman he loved very much, had poured poison through the phone line directly into his ear.

Across the room, he saw motion from the metal blinds separating Bill from the rest of the office. Blake didn't understand why he didn't just keep the window open. He was the boss. The entire floor was the Fishbowl to him. Then again, if the window were open all the time, they could see him, too, like a caged animal stalking around in his enclosure. And God knew what the hell he was doing in there. They had all heard the rumor about what cost him his cushy gig at AT&T and landed him here supervising a call center. The only problem was that each of them had heard a slightly different variation of the story.

Bill caught Blake looking at him and the blinds snapped closed. A little less than five minutes later, one of the in-house lines on Blake's phone started blinking and ringing. Ten minutes after that he was in the office.

*

Lunch would have to wait, but that was no big deal. A certain amount of hunger made him feel on edge, which sharpened his mind and helped with sales. Too much food, too much of anything, would make him complacent and he would slip. The customer may have been the star of the show, but he was also an opponent, at least in the beginning.

Bill looked at him from across the varnished wood surface of his kidney-shaped desk. He leaned back in his CEO chair ribbed in cognac-colored leather cushions. Behind him, the shelves were filled with awards and books. There was a Toastmasters trophy wreathed in golden garlands, several self-help and self-improvement books, covers graced by wide-smiling men in expensive Italian suits with ionized teeth. Chief among the artifacts on the wall behind Bill was the most dear memento of his long career as a salesman, a stub from a ticket to a Police Athletic League charity event he had sold as a kid pounding pavement door-to-door, matted on a black felt background, encased in glass.

"You know why you're here?" Bill leaned back in his big comfy leather seat.

"Because I'm in trouble?" Blake leaned forward, the wood of the chair he sat in creaking and wobbling so he felt like it was going to fall apart and leave him with an ass-full of splinters.

Bill filled his cheeks with air and let loose a series of sounds somewhere between blown raspberries and watery farts. "Hell, if you do any better, *I'll* be in trouble because you'll have my job."

Blake stowed the smile, let the compliment warm him like a fireside blaze heating the weary bones of an old dog. It felt good to be good at something, something legal that wasn't killing him or killing everyone who got in his orbit.

Bill spun around to his high steel cabinet. He pulled open a drawer, riffled through the folders, digging for his duplicate copy of Blake's sales record. After he found it, he pulled the file, shut the cabinet, and spun back around.

Blake glanced at him. Bill looked like a Bill, with the haggard air of a middle-aged salesman who had a crick in his neck from looking up to see who got promoted above him this time. At one point he had been a big cheese, but whenever things went south for him, they never ever went north again. His eyes had a watery quality. He looked like he stowed away a lot of physical pain, maybe acid reflux, and a lot of the other kind, like some great catastrophe going on in his private life to mirror the failure in the professional one, so it was only a matter of time until the loop between hell at work and hell at home closed shut and he started shooting. They talked about the potential for him snapping in the office (a couple morbid punters even had a betting pool going on it). Blake only hoped that when he squeezed the trigger, he did it to himself instead of going postal and blasting rounds into the thoroughbred stalls or the Fishbowl. Then again, they had so many bad days in the Fishbowl they might welcome death.

Bill studied Blake's wins, his maybes, his no's. He whistled under his breath. "If you get commitment to move on these question marks, you're going to break your own record, and get the year-end bonus."

"Yes!" The joy he'd been hiding broke forth. He winced from the lack of professionalism it showed, but then Bill smiled too, and he felt better. He could put a down payment on a car, take Jenda out to dinner, maybe surprise her with a couple glossy illustrated coffee table books filled with mermaids and naiads and seahorses moving around in Atlantean underwater cities.

"Got a new kid coming onboard tomorrow. He'll start out in the Fishbowl. Think you can show him the ropes?" He gazed at Blake with eyes ringed in skin that looked like saddlebag leather.

"Sure."

Bill nodded. "I understand it's kind of counterintuitive, maybe a little unfair, to take the best salesman and punish him by making him work there again."

Blake shook his head. "Not at all. I love the challenge of it."

Bill smiled at him, looked like he could reach across the table and embrace him like a son made good.

"Plus," Blake said, "Mama said life's not fair."

"Mama was right." The smile was still on Bill's face, but the greyish eyes encased in the dead flesh were colder. He went back through the drawers behind him, head down so that his bald spot stared Blake in the face. He had a cranium shaped like a honeydew melon. It was even the same color, especially in the blanched fluorescence, so much so that if he were to hide in a pile of produce, Blake would have trouble distinguishing his head from the melons.

The boss spun back around, spoke again, breaking Blake from his reverie. "He's coming to us along the same route as you did, diversionary detox and drug court."

That leached the pride right from Blake's bones. He squirmed in his creaking chair, sighed. He saw himself as he was now, healthy and employed, angular jaw filled out and strong since dope no longer had him in its hold; his green eyes alert, russet hair neatly parted to the right. Then he saw the mugshot floating around online again, just waiting to be discovered in a Google Images search, like the disembodied head of some cackling ghost in a horror movie. The Telltale Mugshot, the Hessian Horse Addict.

Dammit.

Bill cleared his throat, squirmed, seemed to realize he made some kind of faux pas. He had to say something to cut the tension, but couldn't quite get the words out, for fear that what he said might make things more awkward. "We all have a past."

Now he appeared to squirm, and Blake had to avert his eyes. Blake nodded. There was nothing else to do, as he felt paralyzed from the awkward pall settled over the room.

"Well," Bill said, clapping the book shut. "Time to chase a nickel."

And like that, the weight lifted. Bill swiveled in his chair and put the documents away in the drawers of his cabinet. Blake stood, his ass aching from the weak support of the chair. Some employees, especially those called in for a chewing out, called it Old Sparky. But Blake had a hunch that the electric chair in a modern death house was probably more comfortable.

Bill spoke one last time just as Blake reached the door and grabbed the brass knob. "We're going to be switching concessions soon. The new one's-"

"Eucalady, I know." Blake took his hand from the door, turned, grinning wide. "I read the newsletter and I'm doing some research after work today."

Bill shook his head, did that sotto vocce whistle again. "You're on it, doggonit."

TWO

Nothing could compete with heroin, but this came close, lying in bed with Jenda beneath the goose down comforter on a chilly night. They had kicked the week's ass and had the weekend with each other. Even better than having it with each other, they had some of that time to themselves. That was the key to a successful relationship. The part that was more science than art. If a guy or a girl could not do their own thing for at least a few hours a day, if the other person needed them and nothing else, things got too weird, too clingy. The dynamic got all kinds of screwed up.

But they could sit in the same room with each other, be in two different worlds (her doing her artwork and him watching a fight on the tube), and both of them could be happy with their own hobbies and the mere presence of the other. Blake thought this could work, unlike every other relationship he'd had.

Jenda looked down at her sketchpad, the tip of her tongue spearing out between the gap in her teeth the way it sometimes did when she was deep in concentration. Her hand moved as if possessed, the colored pencil shading in rays from the sun in the corner of the kingdom's sky as it poured yellow light over the towers and ramparts. She licked her thumb, applied a smear of spit to the battlements, smudging so she wouldn't have to do anymore freehand shading. She held the pad back from herself, studied the bold outlines of her new fantasy empire. "Needs a dragon." She turned it around to show Blake. "What do you think?"

His eyes were on the screen, his mouth open. On TV two guys fighting like kickboxers hopped up on PCP battered each other. They pushed each other into the hard links of the cage, causing the wall to budge so they looked like a school of fish trapped in a net.

"Baby, can you stop watching those two Cro-Magnon work out their latent homosexuality and give me some much-needed encouragement?"

"No more psychology courses for you," he said, not taking his eyes from the action.

"Please." She put some pout in her voice, tapped his back with her bare foot, and his muscles turned to jelly. He turned to her, his will half-broken with lust. But the promised sultriness was out of the eyes and voice.

"What do you think?"

She held her city out for him to observe. He moved closer, turned away from the screen. The crowd roared from the TV, which meant someone had probably gotten KO'd. But the painting and the woman had him rapt. He admired the Tolkienesque spires and crenellations splashed with bright sunlight. "Those towers are penile."

"Are not."

"You started it. Calling my fighters gay."

He looked back toward the screen, saw his hunch confirmed. The smaller Filipino fighter was out cold, a lump on his skull as if he had taken a headbutt from a rutting ram. His victorious opponent stretched out his arms and roared, displaying a mouthpiece embossed with a set of vampire fangs.

"Bla-ake." She stretched the syllables in his name as badly as his mom did, but it was different.

"Jen-da! I thought you like to at least like to look at their ink? Don't the fighters have good tats?"

"Not when they're all covered with blood like that."

"Alright." He took the sketchpad from her, studied the grace notes he'd missed when distracted. The detail on the main castle's outer fortifications was truly stunning, the slightly Ottoman cast of the minarets topped by golden, crescent moon finials. "Jesus, Jenda. Are you going to send this in?"

"I'm scared to."

"Of rejection?"

She nodded, took back the pad, as if she regretted showing it to him.

"Rejection isn't what happens to you. A 'no' is what happens. Rejection is what you feel. And it's your choice."

"That's good," she said. "I like that." She flipped over on her stomach, causing her butt to quake like a waterbed slapped hard. "Give me some more good advice."

He ran his hand lightly along the contours of her ass, feeling its plumpness the way a proud farmer checks the progress of a pumpkin in his patch.

"Here's one I used to get over my fear of cold calling."

"Did you come up with it?"

"No, they taught it to me in orientation."

"Shoot," she said, and sketched while she kicked her feet in the air behind her as if working the pedals of an invisible bike.

"You make up the worst, worst-case scenario of what could happen if you screw up. But make sure it's something over the top."

"Like what?" Her legs moved faster now. She felt antsy, he knew. She wanted heroin, but couldn't have it. That left sex or ice cream, maybe both, and he would be fine with both, too. In either order.

"Like you say…" He paused, reframed it for her world. "If I send in my artwork to the competition and the book cover designers don't choose it, they'll send a dragon to my house and it will breathe fire on me and destroy the whole town with its tail."

She giggled. "That's insane."

"I know. That's the point." He waited for it to sink in. "Now you know you have nothing to worry about. Is a dragon going to come kill you if they don't accept your artwork?"

"No." She continued kicking her feet.

"So, what are you worrying about? Send in the castle." He pulled her purple silk underwear down slightly, planted a kiss on her left ass cheek.

"You're right, babe." She reached over to the end table beneath which Soren the Siamese watched them with eyes of sphinxlike jade. The cat sometimes gave him the creeps, but it was important to Jenda. He liked dogs, usually mutts, but he didn't need an animal in his life the way she did. He hadn't been done as dirty by the world of Men ("Men" required the capitalization when he thought of it from her perspective, especially after hearing some stories she'd told).

After setting the sketchpad down, she turned over, surprising him with a face reddened from silently weeping. "Hold me."

Her arms came out to him and he put his hands around her back, rubbing in small concentric circles that widened from the nape of her neck down below the straps of her bra. He placed his head between her bell-shaped breasts. The cleavage pushed up from the lace of her balconette bra and pressed against the fabric of her t-shirt.

He sent a signal from brain to lower body to kill the erection, but it wouldn't die. He closed his eyes, took a deep breath, held her tight until she finally sensed that he needed her to hold him as much as she needed him to hold her.

"Fuck," she said, sniffling as the last of the tears dried on her cheeks.

"What?"

"Nothing," she said.

He didn't press, changed the subject. "You want some ice cream?"

"You trying to fatten me up?"

"We must preserve the butt at all costs."

She laughed, the sadness gone from her voice, gone from the bed where they lay. At least for the time being.

"Okay." She had spoken so softly he thought he might have imagined it, or conflated her voice with the soughing of the wind outside the window.

He looked at her. She nodded, eyes slightly averted as if she were ashamed he had seen her cry.

"I'll get it." He stood up.

"Can we watch a horror movie?"

He shook his head, but said, "Sure," adding as he went, "I don't understand how you can't watch a fight, but you can watch some monster bite a chunk out of a woman's breast."

"The monster's not real," she shouted to his retreating form as he made his way from bedroom to kitchen. "And the breast is prosthetic."

He opened the freezer, got hit with a gelid gust of icy air that came to him in tendrils, as if presaging the white spirits that would soon haunt their TV. He looked inside the hoary interior of the freezer. There was green tea ice cream, some cookie dough ice cream, and a gallon of the store brand cherry cordial.

"Babe…" He left the freezer door open, walked back into the bedroom. He'd come back here to ask which flavor she wanted, but now it might be best to hold off. She'd fallen asleep, a slightly mischievous look on her face as she slumbered with Soren coiled in front of her (and cockblocking him).

He could have moved the cat, but figured it best to crawl into bed behind Jenda, press his mouth against the nape of her neck and admire the fishtail of the massive koi tattooed on her back, occasionally fitting the links of her necklace between his teeth like a baby working its pacifier.

Blake curled up to her as best he could without displacing the cat. He fell asleep and dreamed he was an armored knight trying to reach Jenda in a grey stone castle where an evil wizard held her captive.

*

Looking out of the window of Telesolutions at Hope Ways was like gazing from the shores at shark-infested waters. The addicts, jittery and lined up out front, stomped their feet in the cold, and concealed their hands in the sleeves of their flannel shirts. They shared smokes and traded war stories, casting nervous glances toward the vest pocket park or the bus stop where they could sneak off and cop a bag if the waiting list at Hope Ways was too long. It was everything Blake had escaped, and something to which he never wanted to return.

The window was a bit of a booby prize with which to punish him as top seller, but it was still a window, and the other thoroughbreds envied him.

"I'll take your spot for you." Donna's sweet voice came from his left, the softness of her tone at odds with the threat made.

"The hell you say." Blake didn't bother looking over.

She stood up and draped her long nails appliqued with palm trees over the grey partition wall separating her from Blake. "Think about it." She glanced toward the Fishbowl, showing him the cinnamon-colored shape of the bun styled on the side of her head, curling like a nautilus around her ear. Blake glanced with her, looking across a field of carpet threadbare as the felt on a shabby pool table, toward that accursed corner from which he had clawed his way free. "You going back there's gonna put the whammy on you. You'll fall behind."

"He's exempt from his quota while he's training this fine gentleman." Bill had snuck up on them with the new guy in tow. Bill sported his red-tinted specs, the oval frame and the thin gold wire making them look like a pince-nez.

"Bill, you're trying to put the whammy on him."

Bill shook his head, tapped the gold bridge of the eyewear. "The specs, Donna. What do they mean?"

She tried to conceal the eye roll. "Rose-colored glasses."

"That's right. You can shove all the negativity you want my way, but I see right through it."

He turned his attention to Blake. Donna sat back down, disappearing from view behind her grey wall. "This," Bill said, "is Michael Tash."

"Mikey." He stuck out his paw and Blake shook it, the skin on the palm so clammy he had to suppress a shiver when they clasped. But he didn't hew to the school that said a handshake said a lot about a man (his uncle was quite trustworthy but had a limp grip on account of a work-related accident).

"Blake," Blake said. "I'm a salesman here."

"He's being modest," Bill said, taking his glasses off to clean the lenses. "He's our top seller."

"For now."

Bill turned toward the sound of Donna's voice and then returned to the matter at hand. "You'll start out over there." He held out his arm toward the other side of the room, where mostly stoop-shouldered men in unstarched shirts and wrinkled slacks muttered low. The Fishbowlers occasionally cast around furtive glances, as if talking to their mistresses on phones while their wives were possibly within earshot.

"You listen to him," Bill said, "and you'll be over here in no time."

"Or Blake will be back over there."

"Donna," Bill said, more weary than snappish. He returned her eye roll even though she couldn't see it, knowing she could hear it in his voice.

"Let's go." Blake stood up, chiding himself for not doing so when Bill came over. The brain was more active when one stood.

Blake took the lead and Bill headed back toward his office, immune to the grim surroundings behind the veil of red glass.

"This your first time doing calls?" Blake walked down the line, went to the last station in a row of scuffed bolt holes with Formica desks.

"Nah, I did a little in Federado. They had us trying to get people to change plans."

Blake stowed his surprise, swallowed hard. He didn't want to judge and had only caught a break on doing time when he got diversionary drug court. But the federal jail system was a different world, and a big deal. He looked closer at Mikey Tash. A receding hairline belied his youth, and the thinning on top accentuated the egg shape of his head. He was beetle-browed, as if the outcropping of his forehead were weighing his eyes down. It gave him a scowling look that was not so much sinister as resentful. He grinded his jaw hard enough to make a creaking sound. The tic suggested coke may have been his drug of choice and that a couple hard all-nighters had rerouted his synapses so that even if he stayed clean, the call to coke would always be there. Blake gave him a month, chided himself for his cynicism, thought he could have done with his own pair of red glasses, as corny as they were.

Mikey sat down, stretched, displaying a longish neck that looked like it could extend to ostrich-like dimensions if he kept going.

"This is your station."

"I feel like I'm back in seg."

Blake ignored that, pointed to the old white phone and the black binder with its torn laminated cover. "These are your leads."

"Collections, right?" He didn't sound confident, but at least they had briefed him.

"Yup." Blake nodded, hesitated. "Did you read your scripts?"

"Oh, yeah."

Blake pointed at the red button on the phone. "If someone is ready to pay, you hit that button and they'll pass through to the suite upstairs where credit cards get processed." He lowered his voice. "We can't do that here for obvious reasons."

"Too bad." Mikey snorted.

Blake ignored that, realized that most of the interactions he had with Mikey would be short, because they would consist of him telling Mikey what to do and ignoring Mikey's replies.

"Do you have questions?"

Mikey tried the swivel mechanism on his chair, got a creak followed by a crack as the adjustable base dropped him a foot. "Shit!"

A hush passed over the Fishbowl as several marketers stopped to see what was the fuss.

"Some advice," Blake said, because Mikey didn't have questions. "Record yourself going through the scripts at combat speed. Then listen to your voice. Count the amount of times you say 'um' or 'uh.' Try to cut down on that. Work on it here and then when you get home, try-"

"Yeah, I do got one question, actually." Mikey pointed toward the break table, a u-shaped harvest gold Ikea knockoff. "What's with the toilet bowl?" His smile was wide, but the eyes didn't light up in time with the grin, so it seemed as if by trying to smile he was engaged in an act that went against his nature.

"Oh." Blake waved dismissively but walked over to the table and the little faux porcelain novelty bowl, happy that Mikey took an interest in something. "This is where the hard cases get tossed."

Mikey squinted, seemed genuinely interested, so engrossed that he tried to swivel again, forgetting the chair wouldn't comply. "You mean deadbeats? People who won't pay?"

"No." Blake shook his head, played with the tattered pieces of paper overflowing from the bowl. "Those get forwarded for a 'credit hit.' That's what we call it when debt collectors like us, or like I *was*," (he had Eucalady to sell) "give up and your three credit bureau score takes a hit."

"I doubt those people give a shit." Mikey laughed, and it was clear whoever "those people" were, he included himself in their number.

"No, but maybe they will if they ever want a good job, or a car. A house." He was still thinking about the car, nothing special, a black Jetta with some miles on it, but not so many that when he took Jenda on a cross-country trip, he would sweat every time he glanced at the odometer. The engine didn't have to purr, so long as it didn't growl so loud he couldn't hear Jenda and she couldn't hear him.

"So, if those aren't deadbeats," Mikey said, waking him from his stupor, "what are they?"

"Some are people who probably want to pay, but kept putting it off. Maybe they forgot. Sometimes they're people who gave the callers here a really hard time. Maybe threatened them, screamed, something like that." He'd had a masturbator and a couple of other crazy anecdotes he could tell. But all those stories might have been a little strong for Mikey's Day One, even if he had been in prison.

The grin was still on his face, so wide it finally looked like it might belong there. "Can we try one?"

Blake fought the grin as it crept across his face, and his eye twinkled. He looked over toward Bill's office. The wall of slats in the blinds was unbroken. Then he glanced over toward the thoroughbred stalls. He half-expected to see Donna moving her beaded bamboo lumbar seat cushion into his swivel chair, but his spot in front of the window was still empty.

He looked back at Mikey, shrugged. "Sure, what the hell." Then he reached into the Toilet Bowl and picked out a piece of paper.

*

"Gabriel Paz." Blake cracked his knuckles, remembered something Jenda told him she read about how that might be bad for him. He rolled his neck from left to right, set the piece of "toilet tissue" on the Formica desktop of Mike's workstation. Mr. Paz was roughly six-thousand dollars in arrears. In about three weeks' time the account would expire, and they would report him as lost to permanent delinquency.

Blake dialed, looked over at Mike, who hovered close to him like a faithful manservant keeping close to his master.

"Never threaten, for one." Blake held up a finger after dialing the number. "There're no debtors' prison, so there's no point."

"Hell." Mikey shook his head. "If there was a debtor's prison I'd have been there a long time ago."

"We all would." Blake's smile was a little wistful. He had beaten most of the demons of his past. Now he just had to banish that specter and he would be a free man. Hell, if he pulled that off he could get a car on credit, not even worry about the bonus (though he would get that, too).

"Yeah, hello?" The voice sounded laid back, a drawl that belonged to someone who spent a lot of time chatting up women. Sonority was hard, tricky to talk against (talking "with" might come later) but it was always a fight at the get-go.

"Mr. Paz, this is Blake Seever. I'm a collections representative calling to let you know-"

"You motherfuckers already gave me final notice like a week ago! You got your wires crossed, carnal. Can't squeeze blood from a turnip."

Blake cupped the mouthpiece, didn't even wince. He spoke rapidly to Mikey. "Imagine you're talking to your best friend."

He returned his attention to Gabriel. "I hear you." Blake tried to spin before he remembered the chair didn't work. "Actually, man…" He lowered his voice, making it seem like this was confidential, that he shouldn't even be doing this, but was taking a last chance. "They wanted me to just pass your file on, after which they'll start a lawsuit proceeding. If you make a payment, any kind of payment, that process starts over from the beginning."

Mikey watched, engrossed, his claylike brow so furrowed it looked like his eyes might be closed. But when Blake glanced up at him, he saw he was soaking it up. "Otherwise."

"Bro." Gabriel's soft voice lowered to a near-whisper, and Blake had to strain to hear. He realized this might be a technique, that the guy might even play from the same book as him. "I got two felonies, man. Me and the square world are finito, either way."

"I don't know if I'd give up yet." Blake felt something buoy him, lift him up as he realized he didn't have to pretend, go oleaginous and all *I feel your pain* in a way that would make him need a shower as soon as he stepped into the apartment where Jenda waited for him (hopefully in the mood for that ice cream, horror movie, and sex she had foregone while weeping last night). This guy had screwed up, just like him. Sure, two felonies meant he had blown it more royally, but maybe he didn't have the advantages that Blake had going for him when he got popped; the lawyer his mom sprang for, the character witnesses. Some of the neighborhoods around here were Lord of the Flies on bath salts, kids on gold-bodied lowrider bikes risking their lives to graffiti a stucco wall in the wrong neighborhood, the closest thing to a role model they had a guy who lifted weights, owned a pit-bull (that looked like he somehow lifted weights too), whose idea of romance was trading a few phials of misery for sex from a girl desperate to stop the shakes.

"I ain't giving up, bro. But I got other obligations ahead of that, you feel me?"

"I understand." Blake had paused before he said that, almost replied, *I feel you* before realizing how corny and inauthentic that would have sounded coming from him, like a guidance counselor trying to relate to the kids in their own lingo. Not only didn't people want to be hustled; they knew when they were being patronized.

"Tell me what you've got to take care of ahead of this, and how long you need." He looked across the grey carpet spread over the office. The carpet hadn't been cut right, and it curled along the edges of the baseboard running the length of the room.

"I got a girl with my kid. I don't pay her every month, it's a bench warrant. I'm back on the chain and headed to county in an orange jumpsuit. You feel me?"

"Yeah."

Mikey looked on, eyes moving from receiver to earpiece as if he somehow might follow the volley of the conversation that way.

"Then I got restitution for the second felony. I'll be paying that shit down for the rest of my natural born life."

"See, though." Blake tried to spin again, his senses so used to the swiveling his body couldn't accept that the chair had no give. "You already know how a payment plan works."

"Look, man. I gotta roll. Just tell your boss or whoever you tried and move on. Alright?"

"Sure-"

The phone slammed on Gabriel's side with a finality that caused an acoustical squelch in Blake's ear. He'd had some "no's" recently (even the best salesmen had to deal with them), but it had been awhile since someone had hung up on him. Not only that, but when most people slammed the phone, it was after things kept escalating, so that there was some warning before they pounded the phone hard enough to hurt his eardrum.

This time, though, he and Gabriel had some rapport, were discreetly chatting man to man after a short intro. He would have taken "No," with no problem. Paying the medical bills of some guy he'd put in a wheelchair or giving money to the mother of his child so she could clothe and feed Junior *was* a better use of his money.

What hurt wasn't even the slamming of the phone in his ear. That wasn't personal, and such moments built calluses one needed to develop if they ever hoped to make it in this hard world. The dictionary salesman who gets one door shut in his face so hard the brass knocker catches him on the nose won't get rattled when he ascends the steps to the next house and knocks, despite the inhospitable sounds of a dog barking or a couple arguing.

What *really* hurt about the call was that Gabe (he was already thinking of him as "Gabe" instead of Gabriel) had told him to tell his boss it hadn't "worked" (weren't those his words? Or something to that effect?) The implication being that Blake had not been himself, had been hustling when he had let his guard down to offer genuine sympathy and tried to rescue the guy's name from the Toilet Bowl. But Gabe Paz was content to languish there like a turd, and apparently to get flushed soon.

"You alright?" He looked up at Mikey, with his right eyebrow raised, the chevron spike trying and failing to lift the wrinkled flesh of his brow.

Blake shrugged, smiled and found the effort drained him. "Win some, lose some."

"Man, you were on there for like ten minutes." Mikey checked his glow-in-the-dark Timex to confirm it.

"Winning calls usually take less time than the strikeouts."

"Old boy sounded pissed."

"Stressed, more like it," Blake said, sympathy for Gabe keeping him from feeling pity for himself.

"Yeah, who isn't?" Mikey looked around the office as if his question weren't rhetorical and would get an amen. Then he turned his watery blue eyes back on Blake. "Still, I figure with it being Monday, he's got a right to be in a foul mood. You try back Friday and he'll probably be more likely to pay up."

Blake shook his head, the nerves he'd suffered from the hard pass and the hang-up evaporating. He realized he still had a ledger full of wins, and not only that, but a bunch of knowledge to impart to Mikey, as per Bill's instructions. He looked over toward the boss's office. He couldn't be sure if it was a fluorescent Fata Morgana, but he thought he saw the boss peering between a pair of slats parted with a pointer finger, watching them with his owlish eyes.

He turned back to Mikey. "Friday, everyone has plans, and plans for how they're going to spend their money. It's Thursday when you want to hit them. They're in a good mood because the weekend's still an idea rather than something they're budgeting."

"Hit 'em on Thursday."

He winced on Mikey's words, winced again when he realized Mike had just repeated what he told him. "We don't hit them," Blake said. "We try to reach them."

"'Reach them," Mikey said, though "reach" didn't sound a hell of a lot less ominous in his mouth.

Blake looked up at the clock on the wall nestled in the center of a pillar to which they had applied too many layers of beige latex paint, resulting in thick streaks that looked like melting candle wax. It was eleven forty-three. Seventeen minutes til lunch. He tapped Mikey on the arm. "Taqueria okay for lunch?"

"Shit, yeah! Tacos."

"My treat," Blake said.

"Thanks man."

"No sweat." He stood, his lower back already a little sore from sitting in the chair he had no desire to ever sit in again.

THREE

Something was off when he got home, not wrong, but off. The air in the entryway was slightly hazy, as if a mad scientist had been sublimating something in his beakers. A whiff of sandalwood in the air solved the mystery. Just Jenda burning incense. Except there was something else, that weird feeling when someone moved a piece of furniture and one finally notices its existence for the first time, albeit in a new location.

He switched the strap of his haversack from one shoulder to the other, looked around the confines of the living room, where a secondhand coffee-colored sofa and lime-green chaise longue sat. He moved through the kitchen, sidestepping Soren, who meowed. The cat squinted and there seemed to be hostility in its gaze. Perhaps it resented that people today were too foolish to heed the wisdom of the Egyptians and recognize felines as their gods.

Blake almost said, "Honey, I'm home," but stopped himself. No matter how much irony he tried to weave into the words, they would have reminded Jenda she was living a straight life, something she could barely tolerate. Maybe he would get back to the bedroom, discover she had given up. He walked slowly so his mind could go through the gears and he could properly torture himself.

She could be fucking someone, a man with more money (easy to pull off), a bigger dick (slightly more difficult). Alternatively, she could have slit her wrists or eaten a bottle of Xanax and washed it down with a carafe of merlot. Or (and this was the worst thought of all), she could be using again. Not only that, but using and beckoning him to share in the ritual, that pregame to spiking that was almost as good as the act itself. In some strange way, getting ready to shoot was better than shooting, at least more triggering. He could listen to The Velvet Underground's *Heroin* and yawn, watch junkies shoot up in the latest grimy indie feature (usually unrealistic) playing at the local movie house, and that was no problem. But he could not watch the spoon warming, look at the glass of water, hear the groaning of the butter-soft leather on the belt that coiled around the arm like the squamous hide of a snake.

The door to the bedroom was closed. He stood in front of it, quaking, thinking, or rather knowing, that if she was in there, in her satin underwear, holy midden of a booty propped in the air, cooking dope, he would shoot with her. And he would not even bother to bleach works between shots, plunge the blood of her veins into his own body.

He breathed in, out, put his hand on the door. Turned the cold brass knob.

She wasn't here, though she'd arranged the tan comforter and eiderdown pillows in the way she usually had them when she wanted to watch TV while hanging off the edge of the bed. Her scent was in the air, the heady mixture of tea tree and chamomile that made him think she either worked in a coffee-shop or smoked a lot of weed the first time he met her at Hope Ways.

The patter of hot water splashing against the tiles came from the bathroom, and he breathed again, this time a sigh of relief so deep he felt like he was deflating. He threw his bag on the bed, noticing he had failed to zip it up properly as several glossy pieces of literature for the new product line slid out of the satchel onto the bedspread. The topmost was a Eucalady brochure, a middle-aged blondish woman smiling ecstatically in a glossy photo in which she sat, eyes closed and mind on some distant bliss, in front of terracotta statues of the Buddha. As if lotion were heroin.

He rolled over on the bed, searched around, felt the remote beneath him, a pesky contoured weight like a rock in a shoe, slight but something he had to address or go mad. He picked it up from under his tailbone, looked and saw it was Jenda's cellphone.

His game had been hellishly off today, starting with that time in the Fishbowl. A million little slights and indignities had occurred during the rest of the shift, from pinching his fingers in the door on his way to the bathroom to spilling coffee. And the hits kept coming after work, a face-full of carbon monoxide

("Green Bus" my ass) from the Metro followed by stepping directly into a puddle.

He'd hoped that the Chaplinesque pratfalls would cease once he was home (how many banana peels could the world cast in one man's path?) And though his mistakes here were smaller (leaving the bag unzipped, mistaking the cellphone for a remote), he still winced and wondered what might be next.

One thing was certain. The contents of the cellphone would not surprise him because he had no intention to look. For that was hers, as much as her diary was, or her sketchbook (unless she had something to show him). Jenda didn't pry into his relationship with his mother, the ins and outs of the begging ritual he had to go through to get the money for their Suboxone strips, and he would leave her private life to her.

The phone was none of his business. The phone was-

Ringing. He glanced at the face, nothing more. "Incoming Call: Dracula," it said. *Dracula*?

The door to the bathroom opened, and he shifted, setting the phone back on the bed just in time.

"Babe!" She jumped up and down, the childlike nature of her joy countered by the heave and jiggle of her breasts corseted by the towel tied around her body. She'd swaddled her head in a smaller purple microfiber towel that swirled upward in a spiral like soft-serve ice cream.

"How do you women tie your towels like that?"

"Trade secret." She lay on top of him, still slightly wet but only in a light coat of humid water beads, as if perspiring after a tennis match. "Sorry, I'm soaking you." She pulled away slightly.

"More like dampening me. Don't be so dramatic." He pulled her back toward him, felt the warmth of her body and the heat of the shower, let the erection flower while holding her tight against him. "Plus, I spilled coffee on my shirt today. Don't worry about a little water."

"Oh." She pouted, made a small cooing sound, and the pain of the day died. "Other than that, everything go okay? You land the Boylston Account?"

"Just have some final details to iron out while we sail and play squash this summer in the Hamptons, but it's as good as ours."

She reached over him, glanced at the literature. "She looks quite happy. What are you selling? Marital aids?"

"If moisturizer and essential oils help the marriage."

"I was thinking vibrators."

"The lotions might come in a tube shaped like a vibrator, but I think it's for external use only."

She collected the papers up, swiped them and the backpack from the surface of the bed like a croupier moving his wooden stick across the green baize. It all hit the floor with a clatter.

"Hey, that's my work stuff!"

"Work later," she said. "Fuck now."

He pulled his belt free, forgetting he had once associated it with heroin, thought of it only as something to shed before he could wallow with her in mindless joy. They would escape addiction and the world and the walls of the apartment closing in, landlords, wolves, the past.

"Here." He felt that pebble in his shoe feeling again, the discomfort beneath his back. He shifted, hoped this time it was the remote. He moved aside. She reached for it, looked. It was the cellphone. She lightly grazed the face, saw the name there.

She looked into his eyes, or tried to, as he chose that moment to look away.

"Babe."

"What?" The erection was still there, though he tried to will it away. If it didn't go down and they fought, it would not be on even terms.

"Babe."

"Yes." He rubbed her bare arms, raising little ridges of gooseflesh that he roved over with his fingers as if he were blind and reading braille.

The sensuous touch distracted her, and she pulled her arms away, set the phone aside, turned her attention back to him. She kept his arms pinned down, hovered over him so that her nose and her plucked eyebrows gave her face the quality of a slightly contemptuous sneer, even with the guilt, fear, and the beginnings of tears gathering in the corners of her eyes.

"It's not what you think," she said.

"How do you know what I think?"

"Because I know guys."

He shrugged, or tried to, but couldn't. She still held his arms in place. "Well, I don't know women. So tell me what you're thinking."

"I'm thinking you're thinking I'm cheating on you."

"And you're not." He'd deliberately drained his voice of all inflection, hoping she wouldn't hear the accusation in his deadpan delivery. It was like his salesman's "Oh," a prompt to tease it out of her, if it was there. But if she accused him of accusing her (which he was), he could deny it (and make her look like the liar while he lied).

"I'm doing light dom work."

He squinted. "For Count Dracula?"

She laughed and her breasts, already casting a soft penumbra over him, rose in time with her heaving chest as she giggled. The erection was back, and the blood drained from the brain again. "His name is Doctor Marvin Drakulic."

"Dr. Dracula."

She continued laughing, and he stroked her ear, hoping she would keep laughing, because he didn't want the tears. It may have been selfish, but he didn't want to hold her while she cried. He wanted to fuck her and then eat ice cream with her and then fall asleep with his head pillowed by her ass while she watched a guy with a chainsaw chase around some shrieking girl.

"He's a nice guy," she said.

"Can I ask what light dom entails?"

"CBT." She'd said it soberly, as if talking about her major.

"Computer-based training?" That's what it meant in his world. Maybe Doctor Dracula had her hook him up to some kind of PC with a keyboard that delivered galvanic shocks to his nipples every time she pressed a certain key.

She chortled, and a spike of her pixie bangs fell over her eyes, depending like a sharp icicle. "Cock and ball torture. I put clothespins on his penis."

Blake trembled, trying to hold in the laughter, but it burst free.

"Don't laugh." She let one of his hands go to slap his unguarded chest. "Human sexuality is weird, but don't kink shame."

"I'm not shaming. But I couldn't help laughing a little."

"It's two-hundred an hour."

"I'm not shaming!" He said it a little louder this time. He didn't want the details.

"And I need it, too."

"The money?"

"That, but…" she trailed off, set her head against his chest as if she could hear the surf tossing in his ribcage. "I've been at the mercy of too many guys. They always had the power. When I hurt him, it sort of heals me. Is that screwed up?"

"No," he said. "It's better than you hurting me."

She sat up, placed a soft-lipped kiss on his forehead. "You understand," she whispered softly.

He took advantage of finally having his arms free of her hold, slid his hands around her ass, moving his palms within her underwear, shackled by the satin, a prisoner of her figurative hold while literally pinned.

"I love you," she said, and kissed him on the mouth, opening his own mouth with her slick tongue before he could figure out what to say. He kissed her, on fire, scared shitless.

*

No one in the history of human hands had a smoother palm than he did. He had been rubbing a sample of the new stuff into the pores of his right hand while cradling the phone between his left ear and shoulder, the honey and aloe scent working so deep into the tissue he would probably smell like this stuff for a week, at least. Which was okay, since it was a pleasant smell.

"I just looked," the woman on the other end of the line said, panting. Her voice had sounded hoarse from the jump, and he guessed she was a smoker. That a quick jog from her neck massage chair to the phone left her out of breath confirmed his hunch.

"And does it say chemical or mineral?"

"Chemical," she said.

"See, Eucalady is mineral-based, for the more health-conscious."

"Yeah, we've been thinking about getting something more in tune with nature."

Nature included colonies of fire ants marching into the hooves of grazing animals. But he knew what she meant. People heard "natural" and thought sonorous dolphin song and hiking through cathedral-high sequoias.

"The beeswax and jojoba scent is memorable but not overpowering." *Unlike some perfume in this office,* he thought, looking at the grey felt wall behind which Donna moved the same product (and maybe faster).

"Yeah, I hear you." The woman threw a nicotine lozenge in her mouth. The echoing sounds of the voices of mall walkers resounded from her end. It must have been hell to sneak out every few hours to catch a smoke in the car during breaks from her shift in the mock bamboo kiosk. "Problem is, I move less of the stuff this time of year, because it all has SPF. Even the chemical stuff I'm using now." She coughed once, muttered "excuse me" under her breath. "People aren't worried about cancer as much now that winter's coming."

"They *should* worry." Blake spun in his chair, or tried, but found one leg had caught on a hole newly worn into the grey fabric. He tried to pull the leg free, shimmying along on his chair and struggling like a spider down a couple of digits.

"Stop making that noise!" Donna tapped her wall with her palm-tree covered nails.

He scowled. She made noise all day, or at least sang. Admittedly, he liked her choices (seventies soul, lots of Isley Brothers with a sultry, pleading lilt, sprinkled with some Jackson Five and Isaac Hayes).

But she was just trying to throw him off his game. Get that bonus, take his car away from him.

Blake looked away from the wall, held the phone closer to his ear. "It doesn't matter how much people bundle up. Unless you're in Antarctica, the nose and ears and neck still get exposed to the sun. And those are the places you're most likely to get cancer. And *that's* where we come in. Not only is our product mineral-based rather than chemical, but it's-"

"Shit, alright. You sold me."

He smiled. Back to hitting shots from the paint, no more jinx from the free throw line. "Alright. I'm also going add some spearmint-flavored nicotine lozenges for you."

"You sell those, *too*?" She sounded surprised, as if moisturizing lotion and cigarette substitutes were a strange combo, or perhaps it had thrown her off that he knew she smoked.

"No, these are mine, from my personal stash." Not exactly a lie. The break room still had some sample boxes left from a couple selling cycles back when they had been moving those. They were spearmint flavor, and none of the smokers in Telesolutions (about half the staff) were going to give up the minor pleasure that came with smoking a couple times per day out by the ashcan under the cherry tree. "I used to be a smoker, so I know how it is."

Which was true, except he had been smoking heroin off a loose patch of tinfoil. To add that, though, would have been selling *way* past the close. "Alrighty, Rachel, I'm going to patch you through to our Orders department." He put her on hold, set the phone on the cradle, clicked the orange glowing button that would send it upstairs. Then he moved his hands across his desk, opened his laminated binder, drifted with his finger on the paper until he found "Rachel Gordon, Hot Stone Cabana, Mayfield Mall, LMT." He picked up a pen, wrote, "smoker," then leaned back in his chair, luxuriating in the moment and cracking his knuckles to make it official. He was back.

"You think you're slick?"

He looked left. Donna's face was above the divider, half-obscured, like a nosy neighbor peering over the fence for gossip.

"Don't think," Blake said. "I know." He held up the peace sign, although this time the gesture meant something else. "Got a commitment to close from my last Green Vend and slam dunked my opener on the Eucalady. One more and I got a hat-trick."

"Yeah." Donna snorted contemptuously, pushed aside a tight ringlet spilling from her new hairdo, coiling on itself like a spirochete. "With performance enhancers. *Cheater*."

"What are you talking about?" He glanced up at her. Or what portion of her face she showed above the divider.

"The Nicorette. A real salesman doesn't need to sweeten the pot."

"Sweeten the pot, my left eye." He moved in his chair and extricated the leg of hollow black PVC from the carpet. He slid, spun, gliding. "I already sold her. I was just cultivating a relationship with a customer."

"Bullshit."

"Probably *a return* customer."

She disappeared from her perch at the partition, though her voice trailed after her. "You think you're slick."

"Don't think," he said again. "*Know*."

His phone rang, and he picked it up, not letting his mind wander to the questions it tried to form as he picked up the phone. But even keeping the questions at bay, one imprecating plea got loose. *Don't let it be Jenda telling me she can't do it anymore*, "it" in this context being their relationship, or sobriety, this square world, a square boy like him. Their life together wasn't much, but it wasn't heroin, it was not hell.

"Blake Seever, Telesolutions."

"Blake?"

"Mom."

She started talking, and he tried to listen.

If he had been a hairier and more primitive animal, his hackles would have risen at hearing her say his name. He didn't remind her she shouldn't call him here. She knew that, and trying to argue with her, or even work in a word edgewise, would have been like arguing with a machine. Or even worse, since a machine eventually stopped delivering its message.

"…the crock-pot is for both of you. It's expensive, so you need to use it. Don't waste it. You can eat healthy and cheap, and if you leave the heat on low, you can keep it on throughout the day. But *don't* leave it unattended!" Her voice had risen at that part, as if he had left it unattended many times, maybe even burned down one of their houses, and it was crucial he not screw up again.

"Mom, thank you. I'll keep my eye out for the crock-pot."

"And the updated form for your heroin?"

"Suboxone," he said, under his breath. So far as he knew, all the staff here had come from halfway houses and diversionary programs (Donna was quite open about her struggle with crack before finding salvation), but he didn't need his mother to remind him of it like this. Not here, not now. Especially not while still soaring after that sale.

"When's your next appointment?"

"Tomorrow," he said, stunned that he had forgotten it. *Don't go back to Chaplin mode*, he told himself, *end this sales streak and start screwing up again*. "Ma, thank you for reminding me."

"See, I'm not just a pest."

"You're not a pest at all," he said, voice softening. It was true. The only reason he ever got angry with her was because he could. The rest of the world wouldn't have stood for it. He felt like shit, said, "I love you," and then added, "I'll try to come over this weekend."

"Bring Jena," she said.

"I'll try," he said, but knew that was a lost cause. Normal family stuff weirded her out too much. "Ma, I really gotta go."

"Okay, son. I love you. And I'm proud of you. Being clean, working." He heard the quaver in her voice, could sense the glassiness of her eyes as she tried to blink back the tears. But if he stayed on the phone much longer, too much water would gather in her eyes, and the next blink would cause her to shed the tears. And he couldn't handle the tears of two women, one at work, and one at home (though Jenda had been "up" as hell since their wonderful weekend).

"Bye, ma." He hung up.

"Ah…" A mocking saccharine coo came from Donna's cubicle, followed by the sibilant whisper of an emery board against her nails. "The boy loves his mother."

"Damn straight."

"I called it, though."

"What?" he asked, lulled by the sound of her humming Standing in the Shadows of Love counterpointed by the shush-shush swish of the fine-grained board moving back and forth across her nails.

"You been cheating. Getting outside help from your mama."

"Just file your nails."

"I'm not filing them. I'm buffing them."

"My mistake." He leaned back in his chair, glanced at the clock. Lunchtime. "Think I'll celebrate," he said. "Thai Fusion." He turned toward the wall. "You want anything?"

"Thai ladies do my nails. I do my cooking. And I like Korean."

"Fair enough." He stood, turned, and Mikey Tash was close enough to set a pick in basketball. All his analogies, Blake noticed, were coming up hoops today instead of war, which was a good sign; war was for hard days, sports were for streaks slick as Astroglide.

"Getting our asses wrecked over there in the Fishbowl today." He jerked a thumb back toward the other half of Telesolutions, the fluorescent somehow harsher, making the white dress shirts of the hunched workers look like the skeletons of small dinosaurs bleached in the sun.

"Keep that streak over there."

Mikey looked toward the voice, scowling in Donna's direction. Now it was Blake's turn to set a pick, and he stepped aside, making himself into an impromptu barrier between Mikey and Donna. He felt protective of her, but he was also keeping Mikey from getting screwed up, since she would brook no nonsense, especially not from a new guy still toiling in the Fishbowl.

"You want to get lunch?" Mikey leered, and Blake had to fight the impression that he had misheard, that Mikey had asked him if he wanted to get high.

"Sure." Blake's insides felt like he had swallowed a phial of poison and must conceal the pangs of death from showing on his face. There was always the chance that Mikey had heard him talking to Donna (there was something batlike about the way his ears pointed, as if he could echolocate) and if Blake said he wasn't hungry, it might hurt Mikey's feelings.

"Let's go," Blake said. He made a note to self to swing by Bill's office, brag about the recent victories, make some sales suggestions, and then sandwich in a quick mention that he would take the afternoon off for a medical appointment tomorrow. Bill would know the nature of the appointment, of course, but wouldn't use the "H" word.

Blake walked with Mikey, got halfway down the hall, stopped so that the rubber traction treads on his loafers made a scraping sound on the carpet like a bike tire screeching to a halt too fast. "You go on," he said. "I need to hit the head, first."

"Sure."

Mikey walked down the hall, his posture too straight, as if he might be a robot. Blake turned, walked back toward the desks and chairs and phones where people were selling. Then, he turned to the left, walked back over to the Fishbowl. He approached the porcelain toilet. Just another joke novelty in the office, like Bill's rose-colored glasses or his TV remote ("changing your attitude is as easy as changing the channel!").

Blake reached his hand inside the bowl, feeling a terror similar to what someone rummaging through a box filled with poisonous spiders must feel. A tingling started in the base of his spine.

His fingers clasped a piece of paper, tentatively, like the rusty tines of a vending machine claw designed barely to clutch some plush novelty toy before it slipped free. He pulled his hand out of the bowl, heart beating as if there had really been spiders in there but he had survived the ordeal.

He opened the piece of paper, looked at the name and number. It was Gabriel Paz.

FOUR

There was not just a chance, but the certainty that at least one person from Telesolutions would see him across the street going to get his script for Suboxone filled. He knew as much because Donna had told him a couple of times, before adding, "I'm not judging, either. I had my own demons." Then she'd ceased blowing the cuticle grains from her nails, continued hitting them with the buffer, and segued from demonology to Parables. "I don't care how hard you went with the needle. It's a mote compared to the beam I was carrying."

Blake didn't worry about people at the office, especially Donna. She meant well (despite gunning for what he considered his bonus). The bigger danger was running into someone he knew from the old life, the humiliation he might feel as their eyes lighted up as they recognized him. And that would force him to remember where he had been. He couldn't escape it until he escaped the cravings, which, while shadows of their previous screaming forebears, were still loud and surged through his veins.

Thankfully an afternoon appointment meant less queuing. That meant fewer chances for someone to spot him.

He saw only one person he knew on the walk from office to clinic. It was Roll-O, an addict who got his nickname from the county charity ward wheelchair he pushed. He wore multiple blue shaker sweaters regardless of the weather, and fingerless leather gloves studded with little metal balls. He'd been around here since before Hope Ways was a Suboxone clinic. Back then some clients (re: addicts) would get their methadone and hold their Dixie cups of junk substitute in their mouths and then sell the "spit-back" to other addicts too screwed up to get into the program. Rollo had regaled Blake with tales, including the one about how he lost his legs. "Some people thought it was septicemia, but it wasn't." He'd shaken his head, scratched the porcupine bristles of his neck beard. "I got a pinworm infection when I was a kid. Fucker was living in my gut for thirty years and went nuclear one day after I OD'd. Fluid collected in my legs til I got elephantiasis." He'd laughed as he said it, cackled even louder when he saw the horror written on Blake's face. "Paramedics said my legs were heavier than most bodies. Had to cut 'em off just to carry me."

Rollo had been around long enough to remember before Peace Park up the block became known as Piss Park, back before the last of the birdwatchers with their Zeiss binoculars and checklists cleared out for good to make way for the gathering army of the undead.

Blake couldn't afford the juju that might rub off on him if he hobnobbed too long with the legless relic of an evil time. He slid inside the building, walked up to the plexiglass window plastered with hotline numbers for addiction counselling and outreach for domestic violence. The older black woman behind the desk looked up at him, her popcorn-ball shaped fro streaked with more gray than last time. "Name?"

"Seever, Blake."

She looked at her computer, then gazed at him. He didn't have any charm or humorous banter, but hazarded that even if he did, it would be wasted on her. "Doctor be with you in a moment."

"Thank you."

He stepped left, into the waiting room, and looked around once. Just as he feared, the waiting room was filled with beautiful women. He looked up toward the wall, searching for the TV spotwelded there to distract him from them, these sisters of Jenda, performance artists and models with perfect skin and eyes filled with colored light despite what the drug did to the luster of most who used. These girls had track marks and other scars (some self-inflicted with razors) but coverup tattoos hid most of those, the hesitation marks concealed beneath thorny roses and butterflies.

Blake watched the women, some of them focusing on their schoolbooks open on their laps, others tending rambunctious children. Beauty looked like a horrible burden.

"Mr. Seever?"

He stood, ready to go through the steps. "Right this way." He followed the nurse in his scrubs, a man bowed with muscle with a commanding voice and a shaved head. The nurse turned toward Blake once as they made for the office, looking at him with wounded pride. Darting eyes offset his hyper-masculine body, as if he suspected that despite his bulk and gruffness someone might still look at him and ask, *What are you doing in a girl's job*?

"Let's get those vitals."

Blake went limp.

He yearned to be back in his chair at work, trading mild barbs with Donna, swiveling in his groove, with all that accrued technique at his disposal. His tongue would be nimble and not a clogging, sluggish glob of meat in his mouth, like now. Here he was nothing. A suckerfish who needed his mother's husband's insurance plan and the elixir the doctor only dispensed after Blake let them poke and prod his body, and after they forced him to leave his fluids in a little jar. Not only didn't he have any independence; he didn't even have trust at the most basic level. Here not even his piss was his.

Then the counselor would probe his mind, as if Blake weren't man enough to keep his problems to himself. As if, were he to share his problems with the counselor, the man might understand them or somehow be able to help him. Then they would send him back into the waiting room, where he would watch the sadistic sport the world made of the poor and dumb on the boob tube, having them eat the sex organs of weird animals and jump through hoops (sometimes literally on those obstacle course shows). He would stare at couples in canvas-backed chairs on a dais, watch them argue about who would not take care of that wide-eyed child on the jumbotron behind them, based on the results of a paternity test.

And if he took his eyes from the screen, there would be the women whose beauty hadn't saved them, but had damned them. And there would be their children crawling toward the handful of discarded toys left on the carpet as an afterthought...crawling toward the needle.

He tried to get through the steps required to stop the screaming in his blood from becoming an agonized wail in the mind and soul. He closed his eyes and tried to fight off the unbidden image as it came to him. He saw Jenda on her knees before Count Dracula pulling back his black cape cinched at the neck with a Saint Christopher's scapular medallion. He watched her apply a series of wooden clothespins to the white, cadaveric worm that was the count's ancient penis.

*

He left the Hope Ways clinic with script in hand, shuffling past the evening rush as they came toward him. The sun was still up, throwing a soft yellow light on his skin. That and the fresh air made him think he could survive the day, resist the temptation to jump in front of the Metro bus that usually took him home.

Rainwater filled a massive puddle in a pothole at the street corner. It had turned oily, and though polluted, glistened like an abalone shell in a mix of turquoise and purple. He asked himself how poison could be so beautiful, before realizing it almost always was. The options were clear: he could live, barely, or he could do what would eventually kill him, and in doing so he could truly live until he paid the price.

Everything else was a lie. He sensed it, faintly, and knew that Jenda knew it in her bones, too. He could feel her pulling away even when they were skin to skin, not just pulling away from him, but pulling away from life.

He couldn't go back to the needle (especially not when the legless cautionary tale Rollo stood there on the corner, trying to pop wheelies despite the degraded rubber on his Dunlaps). But he had to do something stupid and dangerous soon, or all would be lost.

Blake marched back into the clinic, walked down the hall, toward the beige courtesy phone mounted on a white plaster column. He picked up the phone with his left hand. Then he pulled the number from his right pocket and dialed Gabriel Paz.

It rang once, twice. "Yolo?"

"Hey, this is Blake Severing from Telesolutions again." He had committed a crime already. Using privileged info that belonged to his employer in a personal, non-work-related setting. It was too late to turn back, though.

"Yeah, man. That's *twice* you fools have already called me saying it's the last time. I already explained to some other dude last week that I just don't got the resources right now to-"

"That was me." Blake looked around, glanced down the hall, saw a punk rock girl with a pixie cut walking toward the waiting room. Either it was Jenda or she had a doppelgänger (possible, as she had a "look" and other scenester chicks had it too).

"Wait, that was you?"

"I called you." Blake shifted his weight from one foot to the other.

"So…What do you want?" There was loud exhale on the other end. It was the sound of a man with many burdens, who felt those burdens every time he breathed. Blake felt bad for him, or not bad for him, bad *with* him. They shouldn't be rivals. They should be friends.

"Man, I just wanted to apologize for bugging you, you know?"

"Yeah, no worries." There was hesitation in the voice, the syrupy cholo drawl drained of its molasses.

"And to let you know…" Now it was Blake's turn to hesitate. He started again. "Let you know that what I did, I didn't have to do. I was just calling to explain to you what the risks were if you didn't pay."

"I know! I got *real* risks in my life, man. You think I'm worried about a fucking bill? I got two strikes. I just got out behind a five-year bid! My ass is facing football numbers if I go back to the pinta again. You don't pay your bills in there, you're fucking dead! So, what?! You trying to be employee of the month and catching feelings 'cause you swung, and you missed on a cold call? Go get a therapist or something, bitch!"

"Pay your bills, you lazy fucking…" Blake's blood, screaming for dope, now boiled from rage. The alienness of the anger surprised him.

"Lazy what? Spic? Is that what you want to say, gabacho? Trying to make like you're my friend and as soon as I tell you how it is, all that hate in your heart comes out, you racist motherfucker."

Blake tried to speak, but his lips were quivering, and his thundering heart allowed him only the shallowest of breaths, like a fish flopped onto a boat deck struggling for air.

"You lazy mother-fucking crackers will sit there on your Rascal scooters, busting the shocks on them shits cause you're so fat, and have the nerve to call someone picking strawberries in Oxnard twelve hours a day lazy. Fuck out of here with that!"

The anger drained out of Blake, not forced out by the combative tone of his opponent, but by a desperate need for Gabe to understand him. Getting called racist scared him, too. Like every other white male cubicle jockey, he knew such a charge could bring down the unholy wrath of HR. But what hurt worst was the accusation that he was lazy.

For there was nothing, Blake now realized, that he would not do to get that bonus, to get that car, to find a way not to be dependent on his mother, on his mother's boyfriend, on dope. If picking strawberries could have stopped this nightmare, he would have donned a tattered felt cowboy hat, a weatherbeaten flannel shirt, and gone to work in the furrowed rows of green leaves out there beneath the baking Salinas sun.

Blake opened his mouth, knowing he couldn't explain any of this. He wanted to try, though. He had to try.

But the line was dead.

*

Moths swarmed in the pools of light spilling from the mercury vapor lamps around the Walgreen's, as if desperately willing the lamps to be something besides false suns. Watching the bugs scramble in the hellish pink light only made the crawling sensation worse beneath his skin, and he shivered as he walked through the automatic doors and felt the blast of arctic air from the AC.

"Welcome to Walgreen's." The smile remained plastered on the face of the boy at the front desk with the Statue of Liberty gelled spikes, though his eyes narrowed as he took Blake in.

Blake shivered head-to-toe and his eyes were desperate and wide, blinking as if that might bring things into better focus. He walked toward the back. This would be easy. Just pick up the script, put a sublingual strip under the tongue, make it home. Then curl up tight against Jenda's warm and soft body in a warm and soft bed, sink off into narcotized sleep. Get up in the morning, have a hearty breakfast, crush it with the Eucalady account for eight hours, catch the bus home. Wash, rinse, repeat. Boring was best. And no more thinking of Gabriel, or what he had said.

Employee of the month. As if Blake had been chasing something that trivial. As if he didn't have to endure his own life-and-death struggle, about which Gabriel knew nothing and presumed to know everything.

"Good evening." The pharmacy tech stood behind a plexiglass divider that went from counter to ceiling with a hole in it. The neighborhood was scruffy, "transitional." It had some cool music venues, but some scary apartment complexes where those fleeing the ghetto had used housing vouchers and were warrened away behind venetian blinds missing slats. They lived in apartments in which the sounds of barking pit-bulls and crying babies was a constant music.

"May I help you?" The tech was an Indian woman, eyes brown but shading toward purple, cute and narrow-featured, with big glasses that gave her an owlish look.

"Prescription for Seever, Blake."

"One moment, please."

She sounded especially curt. It was always this way. They knew they were glorified dope dealers, pushing whatever lobbyists could sneak past the FDA's nose. For every grandma come to pick up a blister packet to let her tolerate pollen when she frolicked with the grandkids, there were ten customers coming to cop their dope substitutes or something to give them a six-hour erection.

Except this time she didn't say, "Your script will be up shortly," in the same monotone in which she had told him to "wait one moment." This time she squinted, looked back up at him. A thought flitted through his mind, and he imagined Jenda in her own white lab coat, or at least in her phlebotomist scrubs, and he smiled.

"I'm seeing the script here, but the payment is not going through."

The smile dropped from his face and it felt like whatever muscles or tendons kept his heart in place had snapped, and that his heart was bouncing from rung to rung of his ribs and down into his stomach. "It's not going through?" He looked at her with queasy eyes.

Her expression changed from one of mild annoyance to disgust. She swallowed once, as if holding down bile, blinked and squirmed as if trapped in an elevator with a man who made her uncomfortable. "Carl Wintergarden's Visa?"

She looked at him, stowing the hint of a smile, he thought, her lips curling. Could she possibly be sadistic enough to get off on denying him his dope, or rather his dope substitute? Maybe it was a power trip, her way to avenge the abuse that some male instructor had subjected her to while she was taking courses, a little too touchy feely or simply standing too close as he explained medical contraindications.

He told himself it was all in his head, nothing personal. Or he tried to tell himself, finding that the signals were getting crossed in his body even on basic functions. *Worry about not puking now, worry about having bad thoughts later.* "That's my mother's husband." He shifted in place, looked down, ashamed, hit by the thought that tormented him. *He needs his mommy to buy his dope. He takes the bus to work.*

"Thanks anyway," he said, swallowed, his spit tasting like foam in the mouth of a man bit by a rabid dog.

He turned, walked out, fumbling in his pockets for his cellphone (he was on Carl's plan there, too). He typed a message to his mother, fingers numb from withdrawal so it felt as if he were trying to work the numeric pad with heavy wool mittens.

"Ma, the card didn't work." A demon within him, the drug, shouted for him to type in all caps: WHERES MY STUFF CUNT!!! He knew it wasn't him, except in the sense that he had been stupid enough to put the needle in his arm, and now it would never really come out.

No junky ever got free. So what was he doing pretending? Why not go back to the real mother upon whom he was truly and forever dependent, whose love he would always miss unless he agreed to bathe in it, swim in it til he drowned?

And Gabriel was right. *Employee of the Month.* His insignificant goals.

Blake's heart, aching from withdrawal, murmured. What if Gabriel screwed him, called Telesolutions claiming that Blake had called him and insulted him with racial epithets, and outside of work hours (and from the courtesy phone in an outpatient drug treatment center, no less?)

Blake licked his lips, and it stung his tongue, and left his lips feeling chapped to the point of blistering. He walked up the street. He moved past men in blue chino jumpsuits with their lunch pails waiting for the Metro to take them to third shift jobs, mingling with women in white nurses' outfits, matching white stockings, and white sneakers.

The sweat on his skin felt as if it were congealing into a glaze so thick he would need an ice scraper to remove it. He shivered as he entered his apartment building beneath the torn canvas of the overhanging bullpup awning. He took a deep breath as he entered. There was the bleach scent left from a recent cleaning, the usually welcome aroma of commingled cooking smells. The buttery steam from vindaloo sauce emanating from the crack beneath one door, the rich and greasy aroma of soul food frying in cornmeal from another.

It turned his stomach. Everything in his body designed to hunger for food itched only for the sublingual strip. If this went on, if his mother didn't call back-THE CUNT!- *She's not a cunt*, he told the drug. But the longer he went without Suboxone, the closer he would get to being forced to not only concede the argument to the drug, but conceding his veins and his life and his soul again.

This screaming had to stop. Once again he briefly considered throwing himself in front of a bus. Then he opened the front door of the apartment. "Honey, I'm home!" And he prayed silently that Jenda had done nothing to betray him today, or that if she did, that she was at least good enough to keep it from him.

Or maybe she was in on the conspiracy with the female pharmacy tech. They were in the vanguard of some gynocracy. In the future only women would be degreed and well-salaried and men would be castrated and hoarded into small call centers where they slaved in tiny cubicles honeycombed across some great expanse, like non-reproducing worker ants.

He found her in the bedroom.

"Hey babe." She spoke without the full use of her tongue, mouth perhaps numb from a chunk of cookies & cream dissolving on her tastebuds. Except she didn't have a pint of ice cream before her. He looked closer at her, realized she was talking that way because *her* sublingual strip was in. But she was supposed to be on his plan. Had the card worked for her and not him? And if so, *why*?

Jenda was on her stomach, facing the TV. She wore a black T-shirt whose front he couldn't see, but which he knew carried the jagged, illegible legend of some death metal band with a name not meant to be read by non-satanic eyes. She was not wearing pants and her tube socks ringed with yellow bands were pulled up to the calves, making her look like a girl from the seventies who would be queen of the roller disco. He looked at her body curving there, thought *sex* with what part of his mind the drug had left him, while the drug shouted *drug!* shutting down him and his libido.

"Babe," she asked, "how come I got to go to group to get my script filled, but you don't?"

At least you got yours filled. He stowed the thought that wasn't his, said, "Because some dipshit senator passed a law after I was already in the program saying you got to go. I got grandfathered into the old program."

"That's bullshit," she said.

"I agree." He set down his leather attaché case on the wooden floor, slid his loafers off his feet, and some tension evaporated, enough to at least let him know he could make it through the night.

"Come here." She patted the soft space next to her on the bed. He lay down, let out a wounded moan, snuggled up to her and let her enfold him, cradle him close to the warmth and softness of her breasts.

"Fuck, babe, you're cold! And wet!"

He shivered in her warm arms, and was soon snoring. She stroked him on the neck, muttered "Shhh," several times like a mother putting the final sonorous touches on a lullaby with which she sang her baby to sleep.

Even the drug couldn't compete with her song, and he had a few hours of dreamless peace.

FIVE

He expected to pay for the night's uninterrupted peace with a morning of torment, but his body was in shock, and the pain and nerves were gone. It was as if the demon that screamed for dope couldn't believe he would be brazen enough to deny it not only heroin, but even the meager substitute. It was regrouping, contemplating its next attack.

It was crazy to give the addiction sentience, as if it were one of those little cartoon devils with a pitchfork sitting on his shoulder, but calling it crazy didn't stop it.

"Soren's creeping me out."

He tossed on the bed, ripped from his thoughts by Jenda's soft voice and the play of sunlight breaking through the Venetian blinds in golden bands. He gripped her tight, as if she were a lifeboat in a storm. "What's wrong with Soren?" He held her, looked with her at the cat who stood still with his tail wrapped around his dove-gray coat. She had always been protective of the cat and shut him down when he said anything similar about how Soren freaked him out.

"We learned about toxoplasmosis in class." She paused, said, "I think he's controlling my brain."

Blake laughed, felt the soreness in his chest spread out to all his muscles, like he'd been in a bar fight last night. "I think it's in the cat crap. That's where the parasite is."

"Even better." She snorted, staring at Soren, transfixed. "The cat crap is controlling my brain." She stroked Blake's hair absently, and chills went through his still-sweating body.

"What's the cat crap telling you to do?"

Jenda gently disentangled herself from him, sat up on the edge of the bed. "You don't want to know."

She was right. He didn't. But to be fair, she didn't want to know what he was thinking either.

He stared past her and the cat, at the nightstand where her Suboxone strips sat, visible through the orange translucent skin of the pill bottle. He wondered if she counted them, wondered if he would stoop low enough to steal one of hers (especially when her habit had been big enough to make his heroin intake look like a multivitamin regimen).

More than that, he wanted to know where she was getting the money to pay for her drugs, which would be very, very expensive without his mom's boyfriend's Medicare coverage. "I gotta get dressed." She stood, walked across the room toward the closet. "We've got lab draw practice today."

Needles, he thought. Phlebotomy used different gauges, but they were needles all the same. Thank God she kept her kit in her car.

*

The sounds in the office, the ringing of phones and even the ticking of the clock, struck his ears like screeching vampire bats defending their grotto. There was some hidden line linking his outer ear to the deepest core of his brainstem, a part of his mind that was usually a sanctuary invaded now by every sound. The worst were the human voices, chipper, upbeat, not nauseated or warring with their body's functions, as if their happiness was gloating at his sorry state.

And the worst of the voices addressed him now, brought him out of his foot-tapping and nail-biting misery in the half-cubicle where he had yet to make a single call today.

"Hey, chief." Mikey Tash stood before him, a wide lavender polyester tie going from his neck to below the belted waist of his khakis, a grease-stained brown bag from the deli in his right hand. He smoothed his tie manically, as if ironing it with his fingers. "I'm kicking butt over there." He jerked his thumb toward the Fishbowl, less than twenty feet away, but widened to an ocean when Blake glanced with his storm-tossed senses. "Pretty soon I'll be over here."

A spritz of Lily of the Valley rose from Donna's cubicle, wafted toward them. Mikey Tash coughed but didn't take the hint, waving his hand in front of his face. He stood on tiptoes to see over the top of the partition at Donna, who had used her perfume like a scent gland to ward off a competitor sniffing her kill.

"Hey, Donna. I like your hair."

She patted the edges of the Ronettes beehive, less in acknowledgment of the compliment than to check if his words had somehow thrown her hairstyle out of whack.

"What's up?" Blake said. He tapped his feet as if working a double kick drum.

"Look, man." Mikey stepped into his cubicle, passing some invisible threshold it seemed he shouldn't have been able to break. But it was too late, and he was in Blake's face. "I can see you dying from over there." Mikey turned back toward the Fishbowl, although this time he didn't jerk his thumb.

Blake shook his head, a knot in his neck so severe he felt like he'd used a conch shell as a pillow last night. "I'm still ahead."

"Not for long." Donna's voice had somehow broken through the mace-like cloud of perfume.

"I'm not talking about that, man." Mikey leaned in so close Blake could smell the toppings he'd had on the sub he ate for lunch. He drew back, but Mikey leaned in a little more. Blake guessed this must sort of be what it was like to be the victim of sexual harassment.

"My poison was coke. But I can see you're fiending for something else." He lowered his voice to a barely there whisper. It made Blake feel as if Mikey knew about the thread connecting his ear to his brain, and that he could release a soothing shot of something along that line, if only Blake might say the word. "I can get you right, man. At least til you level off."

Blake tried to shake his head, but the neck was too stiff to comply, and the crepitus crack in his spine felt like a premonition. A warning that if he tried to move too fast or too much right now, something would break with an osseous snap and leave him paralyzed for life.

And because he couldn't protest, Mikey took it to mean he was interested. He reached in his deli sack and pulled out a plastic bottle filled with an unnaturally yellow concoction. It looked like an energy drink, something Blake could drink at his leisure without arousing suspicion.

"Five doses in there," Mikey said. "You drink one each time after you use, and you're good." He leered, and Blake wondered how the hell the guy was selling. Sure, people couldn't see Mikey on the phone, but that leer in his eye was in his voice, too. "This is PCC Oxidizer, man. BALCO Labs couldn't beat this shit." He wagged his head vigorously to ward off any protest. Blake decided he might have made a good pitchman for some cleaning product advertised in spots on late night cable. "I can't use it because it doesn't cover up coke. But with opiates you're gold, man."

Blake opened his mouth, but his tongue refused to obey. It felt like it was ready to betray him, behave like that of an epileptic and travel down his throat.

Mikey turned and walked across the carpet, practically gliding, buoyed on some secret current that carried him like a tailwind just as it pressed Blake down like a header.

The phone on his desk glowed, and he had never wanted to talk to his mother so badly. The dope devil that danced on his shoulder lied, shouted that it was happy to hear from her because it loved her. But it wasn't love. It was the dope she promised, or the dope substitute, relief from the pain that would swallow him if he didn't get right soon.

"That boy's bad medicine," Donna said.

"I know it," Blake said, so buzzed by the prospect of getting his stuff that his tongue cooperated, at least for now. All of his nerves, his cells, quaked in anticipation.

He picked up the phone, depressed the patch-thru button. "Ma!"

"What?" It was a man's voice, distinct, laconic, the tone of someone who would sound like he was reclining in a hammock even making a 9-1-1 call. "Nah, it's me. Gabe. I want to talk to Blake?"

"Speaking." Flecks of foamy spit flew from his mouth. Through the window he could see Hope Ways, see Rollo making progress on his wheels of steel. Blake watched as a dope boy in a black Snorkel parka with a fur collar retrieved a bundle from a storm drain for an addict. He looked at the bottle of yellow stuff on his desk, a glowing alchemist's elixir. He eyed it, feeling like Methuselah gazing on a phial filled with the waters of Eternal Youth.

"Yeah, man. I want an apology for how you handled me the other day. You did me foul."

"You're right," Blake said, heart thumping. He spun in his chair, looked around, stared at the window to Bill's office. Had this made its way across the Boss Man's desk? Did he know? His curtains weren't parted, which was a good sign. "And I want to apologize." Blake's legs were doing the Saint Vitus dance. Maybe if he trembled hard enough, he might exorcise the Demon Drug. Tears welled in his eyes, a lump the size of a glob of peanut butter rose in his throat, and for the first time in decades he had the desire to pray. Maybe he would swallow some pride, ask Donna to read with him, pray for him from out of the limitless depths of spiritual strength only black women possessed. "I've been fighting an addiction here, you know. And…" Blake's voice quavered. His fist came up to his mouth, and if no one had been around, he might have punched himself in the nose, to punish himself for being stupid enough to get clean. Surely dying with a needle in his arm would have been less undignified than hustling his ass and apologizing like a craven eunuch cowering before this ex-con on the phone, or being forced to endure Mikey's fetid onion and honey mustard breath. Rock stars died of heroin overdoses, jazz musicians, too. There was romance in it, dignity even, provided one made sure not to give themselves that hotshot while naked on the toilet.

He noticed he was biting his knuckles to still the quaver in his voice, keep the tears from shedding. But most of all he was doing it to punish himself. He sank his teeth into the skin over his fingers so they left deep impressions, bite marks that didn't quite disappear when he lifted his teeth and kept talking.

"I'm not trying to make Employee of the Month. I'm trying to get a bonus so I can get my Suboxone." He realized that it wasn't a lie, a shameful ploy for sympathy. Screw a car. If he didn't get some Suboxone in his body, and soon, his legs wouldn't cooperate to walk, feet wouldn't do his bidding in so much as pressing a gas pedal to the floor. "My mom's insurance plan won't carry me anymore and…"

He stuttered, lips quivering, face aflame, overcome by a depth of shame he hadn't felt since his first time public speaking in junior high or getting punched in the face by a bully in grade school. If he regressed much further, he would be in a fetal position, in the womb in his mind but literally on the floor of his cubicle. And then, it would be off to the psych ward.

"Fuck man." It would have been two syllables in someone else's mouth but stretched, elongated like syllabic taffy in Gabriel Paz's mouth. "Shit." He lowered his voice "I'll send y'all a payment, man. Patch me through."

"Yes sir," Blake said.

"This way you can get right, man. I was dope sick in la pinta a couple times, bro. Kicking in lockup's no joke."

"One moment, please."

Blake held his finger over the patch-thru, the trembling digit hovering, moving left and right of the button as if deliberately antagonizing him. His finger drifted. He felt like the President contemplating a press of the red button.

He hit the button, and a tension released from his body, the feeling so strong that when he next exhaled, it sounded like a punctured tire letting out air.

Demon Dope was not silent, but it was at least impressed.

SIX

Cold sweats in the cubicle meant flop sweat on the phone. It was hard to tell women about the essential oils in Eucalady Moisturizer ™ while suffering flulike symptoms veering toward something else, as muscles that had been cramping finally seized. It was a sickness as old as dope itself. Seamen in quayside opium dens had done it, hopheads in drunk tanks had done it, and now it was Blake's turn to kick.

But today had not been a total failure. He had landed the plumpest of big fish, and all without angling for it. It had jumped directly into his boat. God bless Gabriel for his understanding. Blake gave himself top marks for doing like Honest Abe had once counselled: by turning a foe into a friend he had defeated his enemy, the man who plagued his thoughts almost as religiously as the dope sickness.

He loosened the four-in-hand knot of his necktie on his way to the bus, left a palm print of sweat in the worsted cloth of the tie after touching it. The bus came to the stop, but he kept walking, preferring to take the long way home in case someone crazy didn't board and start screaming about Jesus loud enough to distract from him sweating and maybe puking.

The sounds of the city at night reached him as if he were underwater, the blaring of a train horn sounding like distant whale song, the shouts from the balconies of the multi-building brick ghetto like gulls cawing above the breakers. His phone danced in his pocket when he was less than a quarter mile from home. He shifted his satchel from one shoulder to the other, reached in his pocket.

He looked at the face. It was his mother. "Mom!" He shouted it, forlorn voice echoing like that of a child separated from his parents in the mall.

"Blake." Her voice went up, as usual, on the third syllable she made of his one syllable name. He winced, told the demon he loved her as it screamed about the merits of matricide.

"I'm sorry, but there was a problem."

Problem my ass. Christ. I'm dying! "Oh?"

His hush puppy caught in the crack between two squares of sidewalk and he stumbled, regained his footing as black laughter from the dark savored his near-face plant.

"We had to cancel the card because it got compromised. We got a new one coming, though."

"Great." He felt like he was negotiating a ransom to get himself out of the hands of men who'd already sliced off his left ear to show they were serious. "I'll make another appointment."

"Can you hold on a couple days?"

A couple days. Time was relative. Could an outdoorsman delay his kayaking trip by two days because of bad weather? Sure. Could a man place his naked palm on the rings of a red-hot burner and leave it there for two days, ignoring the scorching of flesh, the bacon-like scent of skin cooking free and curling into blackened crisps? No. This agony was somewhere between those two poles.

"I'll be okay, Mom."

"Do you need anything in the meantime?"

"No, Ma. I'm good." *Though a bag of dope would be nice.* The plastic bottle of yellow piss that Mikey lateraled him earlier bulged from the weathered haversack he kept slung on his shoulder. Not that he was thinking of using it, but he didn't want to leave it in the cubicle where Donna, or even worse, Bill might find it.

"Okay. We're thinking of going on a Carnival Cruise here soon, but we'll take care of it before then."

"Ma." What lunch he'd been able to consume was moving north from his stomach to his chest. "I gotta go." He turned off the phone, stowed it in his pocket, and let out a mouthful of puke at the curb, aiming for the storm drain. It smelled like watery runoff from a garbage bag and was even the same brownish-yellow color.

"Ew!" Someone shouted from the dark.

"Fuck," he muttered.

"Crackhead!"

Junky, he wanted to say, but cleaning his mouth was more important than correcting some kid who should have been in his apartment doing homework or having dinner.

Blake opened his satchel with fingers twitching like the pincers of a dying crab. His hand rummaged through the material inside, the aphorism-laden motivational pamphlet with the matte finish, his tan moleskin notebook where he kept track of which techniques worked and which didn't. The closest thing to a napkin or paper towel he could find was a brochure from Eucalady. He opened the prospectus, briefly glanced at the elegant women in pantsuits sharing lunch outdoors at a bistro, smiling with white teeth and toasting fluted glasses to their empowerment, the serenity that came with finding the right moisturizer. As if that were the last piece to the puzzle that included a fulfilling career and a rewarding marriage.

Blake wiped the silage-thick bits of food mixed with stomach acid onto the pamphlet, walked it over to the corner trashcan overflowing with a bumper crop of fast food wrappers and super-sized plastic cups from the local convenience store. He felt better, as if when he puked it resulted from an emetic an exorcist gave him to upchuck the demon.

He pulled out his key chain, tried to get the key in the hole in the front door, missing it and prodding the stainless steel housing clumsily. But the force that had been tormenting him finally had a little mercy, and the key went in. He walked up the stairs, feeling like Willy Loman, the dread and beaten down salesman he had always feared becoming more than he feared falling prey to the dope again.

The thought blindsided him, harder than any stickup kid waiting to waylay him in the apartment's foyer building ever could: what if this was it, the moment where he became the cubicle cooler, the one whose very presence at Telesolutions functioned like a gravity well pulling down everything around it? It could happen, as logical as a face-heel turn in pro wrestling.

One minute you're the cock of the walk, and the next you're a mottled has-been who's remaindered whatever feed is leftover after the big red bantams finish pecking up corn to their brainless hearts' content.

Blake stood before his door, looking at the coats of wintergreen paint interrupted with scrims of blisters and bubbles on the verge of releasing wet paint that might flow, suppurate like blood from a wound.

His hand touched the doorknob, the chill of the brass making him shiver. He turned the knob, told himself the day could not hold any more surprises. For if it did, this night would end with sirens and people would read about it in the paper come morning. No, he would not kill her if she was fucking someone else. Yes, he would kill himself. That might not merit much more than a quarter-inch of print in the paper, but the madness of the moment would require he go out with some dramatic flair. He could strip buck naked and walk the yellow line between four lanes of traffic. Run a gauntlet of addicts and dealers, comic relief to give them some reprieve from the desperate motions of their nightmare dance. He'd stare into the pulsing red and blue mars lights of the squad cars, refuse to comply, commit suicide by cop. Hopefully he'd die with his hard-on flopping around in the breeze like a windsock as he went down in a hail of bullets.

He opened the door, a faint patchouli musk on the air. "Honey, I'm home."

"Hey babe!"

A lush orchestral score blared from the TV in the bedroom, and the whine of a theremin confirmed that it was throwback sci-fi and horror night. These were always a nice a break from hockey masks and meat cleavers, a return to mutated giant ants and soliloquy-laden scientists playing God in flimsy-looking labs.

The scientists were a lot easier on the nerves than the slashers, and he sighed as he walked into the bedroom.

He saw the Suboxone sitting on the nightstand before he saw her, the mandarin orange pill bottle taunting him, the sleeved packets of sublingual strips dancing there. He imagined this was what it felt like for Soren to sit in front of a fishbowl for hours, watching those uppity, juicy goldfish swim with impunity in their glass sanctuary.

"Look who's here."

He looked. A man sat there, his torso rippling with muscle, the abdominals sculpted cobbles, not a six-pack or an eight pack, but countless cuts hard as Carrara marble. The man did not gloat, didn't even budge in the slightest, as if even he knew no matter how Blake felt about cuckoldry, his rage would not overcome his dope sickness. And the man's physique promised violence if he tried anything.

Blake looked around the room, thought maybe he could pick up a lamp. If he got lucky, he could brain the guy hard enough to shatter the ceramic base of the light and knock him out. Then he could press his advantage, pull the cord free of the socket and strangle the man to death while the man unconscious.

"Isn't he cool?" Jenda flicked the man on the nose, and still he didn't budge or bat an eyelash. Was this him? Dr. Drakulic? And were they now both making Blake a player in their weird sex game? If so, he wanted no part of it. He could no more drink in the humiliation of another man than endure his own. Besides which, if the guy was going to get off on being humiliated by him too, then the good Doctor had to pay him as well.

Jenda pulled back the covers, revealing the man to be a foam rubber torso. "It's called a Resusci Anne. My friend in EMT school said they were throwing them away, and I saved this one from the dumpster."

"Looks cool."

She flicked the man on the nose again, and his rubbery face barely budged. Blake smiled, glad that she was enjoying her new toy. His eyes darted back over to the nightstand, to those strips.

He imagined him and Jenda in bed two hours from now, the moonlight suffusing their shared sleep in bluish light, Vincent Price leering from the tube with his pencil-thin mustache and arched Mephistophelean eyebrows, elocuted drawl underlaid with menace. And those strips over there, unguarded.

No. That would make him lower than the junky who breaks the deadbolt on his grandma's door and raids the drawers in the china hutch for family heirlooms. He would endure the sickness, kick and suffer, but he would live, and get through this without stealing from Jenda or his mom. And he would keep his shakes and pains to himself like a man.

"Gonna go throw some water on my face." He spun toward the bathroom, turned on the faucet and flushed the toilet simultaneously so she wouldn't hear him puking over the sound of some aliens on TV pulling a farmer up into their flying saucer via tractor beam.

SEVEN

He'd worn the carpet bare below the legs of the swivel chair by turning around so often, trying to figure out what the hell was up in the Fishbowl today. The cold callers were powwowing in hushed undertones, occasionally glancing over toward the cubicle-enclosed side of the house. Some of those looks seemed meant for him, and because Mikey hadn't shown up for shift, that only increased the chance something had truly gone sideways. Had they seen him hand Blake the bottle of yellow piss yesterday? If so, Blake had nothing to worry about. Not only didn't he have dope in his veins, his body hungered even for the substitute that would have registered lower in the urine than heroin.

Then there was Gabriel, the smiling cholo with the laconic drawl whose name and number he had snuck out of the Toilet Bowl, the man he had taken it upon himself to call from the clinic. But Mikey didn't know about that, did he? His vibe was unpleasant, leering, untrustworthy, but not necessarily nosy.

Whatever was going on in the Fishbowl might have something to do with the din over to Blake's right. Then again, Bill had enough problems for it to be something else, maybe something personal, whatever the hell had gotten him fired from AT&T all those years ago.

"Sonofabitch!" Bill's shouts carried from his office, and when he slammed the metal door on one of his filing cabinets, the window to his room trembled hard enough to make the slats on his curtains rattle. Two vinyl strips remained out of place after the curtains settled, letting everyone on the main floor sneak a look inside. Blake glanced over, saw Bill looking out.

Blake looked away from Bill, to the left, heard a telltale *tap-tap-tap* that meant Donna was hammering a new strip of oaktag into place on her wall. She would write some new goals there, after she finished using the box heel of her red Vera Wang knockoff shoe to pound the tacks through the obstinate corkboard.

The waves of nausea had settled into an ebbtide, and the *tap-tap* didn't bother him the way it might have yesterday. He just had to hang on for two more days, go through with his rescheduled appointment, get the script, take it back to Walgreen's and make the pain stop. Or at least slow down.

"Am I bothering you with this hammering?" Donna asked.

"No, but if you're trying to catch up to me, I'm afraid you'll be disappointed."

"You're kind of cocky for a man going through withdrawal."

"That's not what I meant." He gripped the desk in front of him, squeezed the Formica as if it might hold him upright in a world canting left. "You're already ahead of me."

There was a pause from her side. Maybe the intel he'd given her meant she had to make some adjustments on the posterboard she kept on her side of the wall. After the pause, she spoke again, her honeyed voice matched by the swishing of her manicured nails against the felt of the partition as her hand slid over the wall with a foil package stretched out to him.

"What the hell is that?"

"Kratom." It was about the size of a single-wrapped condom from a bathroom dispenser. She tapped it against the partition quickly, as if it were a limited time offer.

"Thank you."

"It'll get you right enough to last for a few days. My instincts as a lioness are to pounce on weakness when I spot it. But..." She spoke in a halting tone. "I don't like to see a fellow addict suffer. And since you don't want Jesus in your life..."

"Not right now." He wished he didn't sound so snappish, but he wasn't himself.

"And you're not black, either."

"Why bring race into this?" He turned the package over, read the indications in the fine print. "You want me to call Pam in EO?"

She chuckled lightly at that, her laughter ending in a long-winded sigh. "Ah, Pam and I are girls. She ain't gonna throw me under the bus for you. No," she said, finally finished pounding her heel against the wall. "I'm saying 'black don't crack.' White's alright," she added in a consoling tone. "But you don't have the genes to handle what I've been through."

"I don't doubt it," he said. "I-"

"Blake..." The voice came from the right. It belonged to Bill. It was uninflected, neither chipper nor stern, the voice of someone getting ready to fire someone. Or maybe call the cops.

"Be brave," Donna said.

Blake stood, took the long walk past all the employees pretending to look at their shoes, their eyes flitting toward him as he walked by. As he passed, their stolen glances turned to outright staring, mixed with murmurs. Then they went back to full volume after he closed the office door behind him.

He walked up to the blue chair that faced Bill. On the boss's desk were various tchotchkes, among them a photo cube and one of those birds that slapped its beak into a glass of water with metronomic regularity.

Bill sat in his chair after Blake came in and closed the door. Then Bill sank into the ribbed pleather of his cognac-colored throne. "Sit down, Blake."

Blake took his seat, heart already somersaulting from dope-sickness like a peristaltic device gone off its flywheel. The steady *plosh-ploshing* of the bird seemed to mock him, saying with each dip of its beak, *Look how reliable this motion is, unlike your own motions, unlike your own life.* The bird goaded him, pausing between slakes of its thirst. *When you get home, will Jenda be OD'd? When you get your next script from Hope Ways and take it to Walgreen's, will the card go through this time? Or will the pretty Indian girl with the big black glasses see that once again your mommy forgot to pay for her baby boy's dope substitute?*

The bird had more questions for him, but so did Bill, and the real world took precedence over the mad chambers of the mind.

"Look at this," Bill said. He pointed toward the papers scattered on his desk, gazing at the printed sheets shamefaced, as if there had been a cake there meant for twelve that he'd consumed alone.

Blake looked down. He saw several names printed on the sheets, information, rundowns and profiles he recognized from his time working Collections. Among the names was one that caught his eye: Paz, Gabriel.

A strange relief washed through him. It couldn't have been the Kratom because he hadn't taken that yet (and he wouldn't until lunchtime when he would attempt to hold down something modest, like a semmel roll or croissant and black coffee).

The relief came from somewhere else. They had found him out. They had caught him, saved him, and he stood ready to throw himself on the mercy of the court. Bill had always been straight with him and now that he'd popped Blake dead-to-rights it made no sense to hedge or equivocate.

"I should have seen it coming." Bill shook his head, then looked up at Blake. His glassy blue eyes were a paradox, dead and yet containing some kindness, as if it were all over for him, but he had some knowledge to impart that could save others from sharing his fate. "I owe you an apology."

Blake had meant to ask *You owe* ME *an apology*, but his lips were too dry and all he managed was a single cottonmouth, "Pa?"

"I should have looked closer at the application for that Michael Tash."

"I thought that was GIS's job?" Blake squinted. A second ago he'd been terrified, but now his heart was halfway back to something like normal rhythm.

"I trusted General Information Services on the background check. Always do." He held up a pointer finger, dead eyes alight with the glow of another man's wise words. "'Trust, but verify'." He sifted through the papers like a palmist rummaging around a scattering of Tarot cards. Then he found what he was looking for, held it out to Blake. The paper had the CLEAR red rubberstamp mark in the far left corner, but the background checkers had missed something apparently, which Bill had marked with yellow highlighter. Blake leaned in closer, the tip of his silk tie falling onto the surface of Bill's desk.

"Wire fraud," Blake said, reading.

"He should have never been here." Bill tossed the paper back onto the desk, shuffled the stack some more, spoke as he stood and turned back toward the grey metal file cabinet behind him. "The dumbass was stealing personal info off the hot sheets just sent down from Processing."

Blake squinted, confusion moving toward something else, something that made his heart pound, but not with fear. "*Today*'s hot sheets?"

"Today's." Bill pulled a file drawer open, selected a replica of a Pee-Chee cardstock vintage folder where he kept info on top sellers. He turned back around to Blake. "If he'd gone in the Toilet Bowl or, hell, even gone through the trash before it had its date with the shredder, he might not have gotten caught. And then it would have been on *me* if a felony got committed here."

Bill sat back down, set the folder in front of him. On the front was a watercolor tableaux of athletes in various poses, a Johnny Unitas clone springing into the air on cleated shoes to catch a pigskin mid-spiral, a ballerina in pink tutu executing a tiptoe pirouette next to a hockey player high sticking on the ice. "Instead, the idiot goes for the ones that everyone would notice missing, hot off the presses." He shook his head. "'Never interrupt the enemy when he's making a mistake.' That was Napoleon, I think. Either him or Ronald Reagan." Sometimes he kept the source of his aphorisms to himself, but this time he had seen fit to share.

"Yeah, but, you don't owe me an apology."

"I do." Bill nodded, opened the folder, looked at the file there before him. Blake had an idea whose track record the boss now had in hand. "Your numbers are *way* down since I let you train that shit show imposter of a salesman."

The massive bald spot on Bill's head glowed as if shellacked, catching radiance from the fluorescent tube above his desk so it shined like an ivory cue ball. Bill looked back up and the lusterless eyes replaced the luminous head. "But you've *got* to get some sales here, soon. Not to get the bonus." For the first time in months, he stared at Blake as if he didn't know him, the warmth- hell, the contrition- of the last few minutes gone, as Bill viewed his star employee with new eyes. He had no choice. It was nothing personal, and to make it personal would have made it harder to fire him, if the time came.

But Blake was not worried about getting fired. He was pissed. The only way Gabriel's name could have come up in the new crop was if he hadn't paid after Blake had patched him through. The fucking guy had lied and Blake wanted to take his head off. Reach *all the way* through the damn phone and bite off a piece of the guy's cheek and spit it out, regardless of how hard an ex-con he was.

Gabriel Paz was only a man, and all men bled, and Blake was going to cut him. The only question now was whether to keep it rhetorical or move this thing toward the literal.

*

Lunch was a gel cap of Kratom, swallowed with some Sprite (the effervescent bubbles held down the nausea) followed by a nine grain six-inch pocket of submarine bread. He wolfed it in the restaurant booth, going to work on it with the intensity of a rat gnawing its way through a cable.

On a normal day it would have been a meager meal, probably wouldn't even have qualified as lunch. But after not eating for so long, he chewed the bread to tiny crumbs before swallowing. It was just a stale Subway six inch roll, but his hunger made it into something else, a baguette devoured by a peasant catching scraps thrown his way by a generous noble. He ate with his eyes closed, saw and tasted golden fields of wheat, ripened oats in an Edenic valley.

It was better than dope, and he was almost grateful for the torture that got him to this moment he thought he would never reach again, where something was better than heroin. Sex with Jenda came close sometimes, endorphins rushing as they both rolled together on the bed toward epiphany, but it always slipped out of their grasp, fading in the most intense moment.

Food, though, remained in the belly. Maybe that was the solution. Get fat.

He stood up from the yellow plastic booth, walked his trash to the container, dumped it, and walked back out into the daylight. The sun no longer blasted him as if he were in the grips of an excruciating hangover, but painted him in warm haloing waves, the late autumn rays making the gooseflesh raise on his skin.

He would have to thank Donna when he got upstairs, although he was afraid that if he started, he might start crying, get so effusive that he began kissing her feet like some vagabond-turned-disciple.

Maybe that was the solution, Christ, now that he was free of the heroin.

Blake considered combining both ideas he'd come up with first at Subway and then on his way back to the Telesolutions building: food and Christ. Become a monk, fat and jolly, weaned off heroin with spiced honey mead.

The lunch break had a different effect on different workers, some slouching into a lethargic daze for the first few calls after the break, others revived and closing sale after sale with pitch-perfect tone in their voices and ramrod-straight posture.

Being halfway sober and no longer sick struck him now as an almost unfair advantage, and as he assumed his place in the cubicle again, he was convinced he could make the next call or wrestle an alligator with equal ease.

Donna had been right to express some doubt about giving him that supplement. The King was back, seated in his swiveling throne. He gripped his binder, marveled at how his hand no longer shook, flipped it open. "Praise the Lord and pass me the Call List."

"Hey now!" Donna said.

"Yes, ma'am."

It was a nice call and response, but he felt sufficiently churched, and it was time to face the world and its wolves again. Get that bonus, get that car. Get poor old Bill's respect again just to infuse him with some of that light which had gone out in him so long ago, left him sad in a way that his gentle soul didn't deserve.

Blake's finger moved over the college-ruled lines of the sheet. His early victories with the Eucalady product, his "wins" and "movement commitments" tapering off to "NO's" and "No answer" entries, one after the other. A supervisor studying the document would have reached the conclusion that either two separate workers had been using this book, or a successful salesman had suffered some great reversal or mishap (cancer, divorce) that caused his numbers to nosedive.

No more, though. He had the telephone number directly above his pointer finger. He dialed with his other hand, noting as he did that the faintest bit of a tremor had returned, and that his digit moved as if guided by a Ouija planchette.

He dialed as if in a dream, watching himself pound the numbers with a tremor. Only afterwards did he realize which number he had called. It wasn't the next customer on the list. And he wasn't back to selling Eucalady. Not yet.

The line rang twice, then someone picked up. "What's good?" A pit bull barked in the background on the other end, and the manic mixture of xylophone and classical strings made it even money someone was blaring loud Looney Tunes on TV.

"Hey, man." Blake didn't know where to go from there, or even what he wanted.

"Yo man. I told y'all I wasn't going back to the halfway house. You want to violate me, go ahead, fine."

"This is Blake, man." He shifted the phone from one ear to the other, kept his voice down, afraid that

Donna might hear him. Or not so much afraid, as ashamed, as if this were some kind of relapse worse than going back to the needle, almost on a par with rejecting salvation, plunging back into this when he had the chance to get free. It was willful, which made it worse than something done out of weakness. "I'm not your PO." He laughed easily, knowing that while a bill collector wasn't anyone's favorite caller, it beat a parole officer.

"Yeah, man, I don't know no Blake."

A stinging hit Blake in the pit of his stomach, softened by the bread and the soothing Kratom dissolving in his belly. But it still hurt. He asked himself if he had told Gabriel his name. Better to explain, refresh his memory a little. "Yeah, man. I know you and I talked yesterday, and I meant to patch you through to the upstairs here at Telesolutions so we can get you on a payment plan."

"Right, man. Oh, okay."

The knot in Blake's stomach loosened, and when he next breathed he noticed how much air he'd been holding in his lungs, his exhale making a scraping sound in the phone that tested the acoustic limits of the receiver. "I think I may have maybe hit the wrong button, or I must not have patched you through correctly yesterday, because your name came up again."

"Yeah, man. The check is in the mail."

Blake's chest ached. Heartburn, he told himself. Not anger. He didn't feel anger at work. Hell, he didn't feel anger at home, or at all. True, his mind was on fire and the weird images were bubbling up in the brain unbidden. Like Jenda somehow cheating on him with the Resusci Anne, imbuing it with life like a voodoo poppet courtesy of some doggerel spell she had heard in one of her horror movies.

He took a deep breath. Usually he found that helped with the stress. This time it did nothing, or perhaps made it worse. To breathe was to drink stress from an incessantly flowing tap, and one had no choice but to inhale.

Unless...

No, he would not kill himself. It would kill his mom, confuse Jenda to where maybe she blamed herself for his act. He spoke through gritted teeth. "You must have me confused with another collections agency. You don't mail us anything. It's a quick patch through. You-"

"So wait? You *don't* want me to mail you the money? Yo, I think you're confused, bro."

Bro had come out in that elongated cholo drawl. He fought the imago of Gabriel Paz being built in his mind, a stereotypical *Ese* with a bald head scrimshawed in blue tattoos of weeping clowns and Lady Guadalupe's. A man inked down to the knuckles who wore a heavy flannel shirt buttoned at the top and some khaki Dickey's shorts and tube socks pulled up to the knees. That Gabriel might not have been real, but the figment was smiling at him, the grin revealing a gold tooth that caught a glint of light from the sun that had been Blake's best friend such a short time ago.

"You only pay us through the office upstairs. There is no way to send us a letter. Another collector may have told you-"

"How do you even *know* I got other bill collectors after me? You just assume cause I got behind with you I owe everyone around town? You think I fall for every bloodsucking RTO scam just 'cause they get someone who looks like me selling sectional couches on Telemundo? Fucking vultures."

"I'm not a vulture," Blake said, feeling ridiculous, wondering why his lower lip was quivering, as if he were back in the schoolyard and cornered by a bully in front of the chain-link fence, the same bully whose friendship he had wanted as bad as he wanted Gabriel's…not friendship, but understanding, his understanding that Gabe needed to show him respect, because he was breaking and if he broke now, it might get bad. Everyone in the office had kept their eyes aimed to Bill's fortress of solitude where he muttered to himself and banged his metal filing cabinets and ruffled the accordion edges of his big manilla bundles. But maybe the time-bomb lay elsewhere. Maybe it lay in him, in his head and heart, which would not give him any peace.

"Hey, man. I gotta bounce. Tell your boss you tried. Alright."

"I…"

Dial tone was in his ear. It hit him like the flatlining of a family member's EKG in a hospital room. He dialed Gabriel's number again, the digits forcing their way into his hand. He pounded the keys, holding each number as he depressed on the phone like a madman playing a Wurlitzer organ, the anger in his veins like steam feeding the keys of a calliope.

But Gabe had blocked his number.

And the Gabriel he saw in his head, real or not, was no longer smiling. It was laughing at him.

EIGHT

He decided not to take the bus home, to instead wear out his shoe leather and burn the excess energy of no longer being sick. Besides which, thinking seemed easier when he walked, and he needed to cop another bag of Kratom.

Cop. He realized only after he ducked into the convenience store he was already thinking of it as copping. Was this the way it was always going to be? He brushed past the other tired workers just off shift, women in housecoats and men in blue duck cloth moving beneath the sickly red sodium vapor of the arc lamps on the street.

He got on Suboxone to get off the dope and now he was on something new, which he wasn't even sure how to spell, in order to deal with not having his sublingual strips from the clinic across the street. Earlier this afternoon, while making calls (and closing a couple of sales), he had thought he was free. But here he was, pinned to the needle as surely as a fly to a mount in a display case.

"What can I do for you, my friend?" The man behind the counter had dark rings around his eyes and wore a guayabera printed with palm trees. Behind him were several oil-on-black velvet paintings of deities in his pantheon. There was the heaven-blue multi-armed goddess with a flaming tongue facing down the elephant with the golden crown surrounded by a radiant halo. Between the two was a color aquatint of the Taj Mahal. It gave the impression the two gods were monsters ready to do battle in the city, and would start by tearing spires off the palace and using them to beat each other.

"Just this." Blake put the grey plastic bottle on the counter, its printed label featuring green leaves that looked suspiciously like those of a female marijuana plant. "And…" His eyes drifted behind the counter, to a part of the store that he'd always overlooked. It was where the mylar-faced cases held cigars sold to be split, gutted of tobacco, and filled with weed. "And one of those." He pointed to the spot next to the cigars, where a bandolier of prepaid calling cards hung on a strand unfurling like a roll of toilet paper.

"International or domestic?"

"Domestic," Blake said, though he would have been willing to follow his quarry to the ends of the Earth, to the snow-covered peak of Kilimanjaro if it came to it.

"There you go, my friend."

Warmth surged through Blake as he took the card, his pills, and his change. The Indian clerk threw "my friend," in there offhand, as a standard bit of parting patter, and yet Blake had felt warmth when the man had said it. He now felt everything again. It wasn't good, this discovering of his sensations the Suboxone usually dulled. The last time he had felt things with the intensity of a normal, non-dope addict had been after the cops in County had draped him in one of those hook-and-nylon suicide smocks. It was a sort of combination catcher's armor, Kevlar vest, and straitjacket. He had shivered as he kicked. He'd stared at the rusty grated hole in the center of the cell on the cold floor, wondering how long it would be before he melted into a pile and slid through the metal grids and down the drain.

He walked now, under the spell of self-hypnosis, toward one of the rare blue box payphones that stood like a tarnished relic, a low-tech has-been in a world conquered by cellphones.

Blake dug in his pocket, ignored the dope man coming toward him, a gaunt kid with a beard thick and scruffy as steel wool that belied his youth. He wore a heavy tricolor shearling, picking a strange place and time to show his afrocentric pride (at night while making rounds to backsliding addicts outside Hope Ways). He made brief eye-contact with Blake. It chilled Blake, caused the warmth he'd been feeling to evaporate.

The kid shifted the band of his grey Champion sweatpants, looking as if he were adjusting a wedgie or the crotch of too-tight underwear. But he was checking the bundles he kept hidden tight to the elastic of the warmups. Blake didn't remember ever purchasing from him, but the look of familiarity from the kid wasn't for him, but for his type. The barely suppressed scream in his eyes, and the telling way he still walked with his palm out and fingers open as if he could somehow dowse for dope dealers as easily as a water witcher finding an underground aquifer. The kid finally turned away to service another customer, but before he did, he gave a slight nod to Blake, or at least it looked that way.

Now was not the time to dwell on what it meant, or if it was all in his mind. Now was the time to put things to rights, exact a bit of revenge on the man he had begged for understanding, the man who had betrayed him when he had come to him in good faith. He stepped into the phone-booth, dug a quarter from his pocket, slid it into the slot.

He pressed the numbers on the calling card, loving the cool and tactile feel of these old, nickel-plated buttons. His nerves belonged to him again, and his hand was steady. And it wasn't just because of the help from Donna (though it was appreciated). Nor was it entirely because of the wins he got with Eucalady after that spartan lunch of a sandwich roll. His hand was steady because he was fated to do what he now did, to dial Gabriel Paz and make him pay. Literally and figuratively.

The phone rang, and he clenched his teeth, tapped his foot, the sound echoing in the tight confines of the booth. It had grown dark so fast, as it did when fall slid into winter. The lights of the city at night had come alive, the headlamps of cars crawling homeward shooting their cones of yellow through the gloam. Neon twitched in front of a bail bonds shop, illuminating a Chinese restaurant with steam clouds rising from its kitchen, the streaks on the plate-glass window so thick that the hanging dressed ducks were half-invisible.

"Yo!"

It was a little girl, a tough voice reserved probably for talking to people on the phone or when someone pounded on the front door.

He almost asked, "Is your daddy home," but realized that wasn't the way to go. Slimy process servers and cops looking to cuff up the breadwinners and send them upstate tried that sort of friendly ruse. He remembered what Bill had said about intermediaries: *Between you and the client, there is sometimes a gatekeeper. The gatekeeper is not a barrier, unless you treat them like one. Treat them like someone who can help you get through the gate, and they just might.*

Blake remembered something his mom told him about working as a substitute teacher in the inner city years ago. "I kept asking them to be quiet, and they laughed. I broke down crying and they laughed." She had shaken her head as she told him, marveling at the nature of man (or kids) as she put a red marker strike-through on a paper she graded. "And then I told them, look, I'm not getting much money to do this. Don't make my life hard and I won't make yours hard. And it worked."

Blake channeled his long-suffering mother (to whom he owed more apologies than he could ever proffer). "Maybe you can help me. I'm in trouble. See-"

"Yeah, what do you want me to do about it?"

"I need you to help me and your dad."

"How you know my dad?" She paused. "You white? You sound white." The emphasis was subtle but clear. He couldn't blame her. White had been mostly, if not solely, bad in her world, cops, proxies for the state, and bill collectors. Except for some fantasy excursions maybe at school where she read about the doings of a bespectacled white boy with a magic wand in some distant enchanted land called the United Kingdom.

"I'm white, and I'm your dad's PO. They want to lock him up because he didn't come in today when he was scheduled. They want to issue a bench warrant."

"No!" She stretched the single syllable out to five. She sounded like the child she was, unguarded, no longer barking at some stranger pounding on her door while watching him through the keyhole with the deadbolt and chain on.

"I'm coming in on my off hours, but if I can get him to check in tonight..."

"Yeah, but he's at work. He ain't here."

Blake paused. From behind him the Metro bus roared, its steel skin glinting in the moonlight. He thought of pulling the door to the booth open, walking out into the street, standing in front of the bus as it barreled down the road and solving this thing once and for all.

Doing dope was one thing. Breaking some laws in a contest with another lawbreaker was okay, too. But he was using a child to get to her father. He tried to conjure the girl in his mind, hair perhaps done up in scrunchies patterned with characters from her favorite cartoon. But then he saw her father smiling, laughing as Blake writhed on the ground in some cell from which there was no escape while shrouded in that county Kevlar tortoiseshell. No escape but to win this contest of wills.

"If I call him at work…" He didn't press, made a chanting sound, a soft hum, as if wondering to himself. "I don't know if it will work," he finally said. "They might still issue the bench warrant."

"Can't you try, though?!"

Fish hooked.

Piece of shit went through his head, but the smiling disembodied head of Gabriel danced again into view and he regretted nothing, knew he would happily plummet into the abyss if he could bring that bastard down with him.

"It might work."

"I'll give you his number. He does auto body detailing over at Sumter Bros across town, twelve to six." She paused, embarrassed, as if the details she'd just spit out had been vomit ejected onto her Sunday best.

"I'll see what I can do."

"Thank you."

"You're welcome."

His skin crawled. He'd won some ground, got a detail, should have felt some elation because this was war and everyone got hurt, including kids. Except his skin was crawling with cockroaches. Beating Gabriel would help him feel better, feel whole, fill the hole, but it might not be enough.

The needle called. The dealer's eyes had not lied.

He picked up the receiver and slammed it down twice. "Shit!" He bit his lip, screamed so loud he went half-deaf in the tight confines of the metal box. Then he left the booth, walking, thinking *Sumter Bros Body Shop*. He imagined Gabriel working there, imagined the details of the face he had been building in his mind, like an obsessed composite sketch artist trying to draw the face of a man who raped his sister.

No one had ever needed to see the face of another human more than he needed to see the face of Gabriel Paz. For him, it would be the face, not of God, but of the more powerful demon that seemed to really control all their days. The one making the people go through their insect-like motions: the drug addicts dancing on the corner; the hand-to-hand sellers in their heavy hooded parkas; cubicle jockeys hunting down people hiding from bill collectors whose voices crawled through the wires like the tentacles of deep sea monsters hungry for prey.

He had a final thought as he started for home, one he was forced to entertain now lest it follow him into dreams.

What if Gabriel Paz was there, at the auto body shop, and he wasn't taking the Vin numbers off hot rides while sharing war stories about a bank robbery or a drive-by with his old road dogs in their mechanics' suits? What if he was really trying to get his act together, just like Blake was trying, or had been trying until the last couple days?

Blake saw him diligently wiping down his wrench with an oilcloth, swallowing pride as his supervisor (maybe one of the Sumter Bros.) chewed him out about some realignment job he had botched. He could feel Gabriel's roiling emotions. His instincts to war over the smallest infraction had been honed on the weight pile or in the chow hall back in prison, where he had been a shot caller. But he would hold it in now, wait for the rage to pass. He would not indulge in his drug of breaking men's faces any more than Blake would put the needle in his arm when thoughts of his mother and Jenda and living with his tail between his legs became too much.

Blake was back to the beginning with this guy, seeing him as a brother across some chasm of time and space, skin and circumstance. But where before this had made him want to talk to him, build sympathy, rapport, save the fucking guy from a three bureau credit hit, all he wanted now was kill him. Because Gabriel Paz reminded him of himself. Because Gabriel Paz was him.

*

It was change of shift at Hope Ways and a group of nurses in maroon scrubs and doctors in white lab coats left the building through the side door. The addicts in front of the clinic looked at them as if they were in the VIP lounge of a fancy nightclub.

Blake recognized one doctor by sight, an MD with a bowl cut that made him look even younger despite the longish red beard. He was the only croaker in the clinic who rode a bike to and from work, and in his office were pictures of him standing in front of thatched huts in rural villages from his time in Doctors without Borders. Blake looked away as the doc pedaled past him on a silver bike, his khaki pant legs bloused with rubber bands into argyle socks. The doctor moved into the darkness of the night, glowing in a wash of red beneath a traffic signal before turning right, then disappearing.

"I got you."

He looked toward the voice, baritone deep and soothing. The dealers apparently had their changing of the guard synced up with that of the clinic, and a new kid was serving the addicts. Blake walked over, trailing just outside the square of sidewalk speckled with glass shards where transactions happened.

The customer in front of him was thin, draped in camo cargo shorts that probably once fit him, and a ragged white t-shirt from Saint Vincent de Paul. "Bet."

The man shuffled off, looking like a scarecrow somehow come alive.

"You good?" The dealer wore a golden Timberland sweatshirt, the hood pulled up around his head so he looked like a monk in an order of crack-dealing capuchins.

"No tar," Blake said. "Just powder Chiva, enough for a car key."

Neither looked at the other, a square of dark and cold sidewalk still between them. "Man…" The dealer gave a surly cluck, looked off to the side as if Blake were trying to sell him Amway. "I ain't got time to be fucking around with orders that small."

"I got to get my tolerance back. Unless you want a body making your storefront hot." He looked down at the cement square, let the dealer imagine how a corpse might cramp his style.

"You just get out of Clarion?"

"Two days ago," Blake lied. He'd been to Clarion (Hope Ways' inpatient sister site) about a year ago, but if the dealer thought he'd just gotten out, he might dole out a bump or two just to keep Blake from getting into treatment.

"Bet…" The dealer nodded, his eyes rolling in their sockets as he scanned the block for cops. He stretched his neck, stepped on tiptoes and stood at least two heads taller than Blake. Blake admired the single motion that dislodged the glassine baggie and let it slide through the band of the dealer's boxer shorts, down the cotton folds of his sweats, and out the top of the tongue of his shoe. The dealer stayed on tiptoe with neck craning, scoped for cops on ride-through or plainclothes on foot, looking like a praying mantis roving for a meal with its compound eye.

Blake folded a twenty, set that on the ground in front of the dealer's foot while picking up the balloon wrapped in grocery bag plastic.

The dealer stabilized the money with the suede toe of his Timberland boot. He reached down as if picking up a cigarette butt or struggling to find a contact, threw his voice on the wind like a ventriloquist. "Soon, I'm only gonna have that Chinese shit. So either get your tolerance back up or don't fuck with me anymore."

I won't even be shooting this, Blake thought to himself, and kept it moving. He stopped at the curb, waited for the light to change. Then he jog-trotted across the street and started for home.

Maybe he would unravel the bundle and toot it to the head, feel the heroin course through his blood and bring him the warmth of a second babyhood for an hour, but more likely he wouldn't touch it. He would keep it in his pocket, play with the dope the way it had played with him, show it less mercy than Soren batting around a little mouse with its poor brain addled from toxoplasmosis.

After he got Gabriel's work phone number, he had expected to feel the rush of a deal closed, only to feel something else that made him finally understand what Jenda had been talking about. "For a lot of working girls, heroin is for when you still don't feel clean, even after the shower. It washes the dirt of the day right out of you, no matter how disgusting it was."

He was sleaze, leaving mucilage behind him, and heroin was the salt. Sure it would kill him, but that was kind of the point.

Blake fought that thought, returned to the one he'd had going into the deal. He put some bop in his step, a spring that made him take each square of sidewalk in two strides at the most. He would show the dope who was boss. No more would he have to stare out the window of Telesolutions and wonder when the weakness would overcome him, or when the beeline he usually did for the bus stop would devolve into a detour back to the dope man. He had already made that detour and would no longer let the drug control him, nor would he fear it. He would let the dope sit there, the glassine bag rubbed worn like a worry stone in his right pocket.

It was his slave now, not the other way around. He took his hand out of his pocket, walked alongside the corrugated metal sheets that formed a curtain wall around the junkyard on his left. Stacks of subcompacts and hatchbacks lay in cubed mounds, the bark of a feral dog keeping vigil coming from the other side. *I must be like the dog*, he told himself, *vigilant to the point of viciousness*, unreasoning and adamant in the goal of not touching the dope so near-to-hand.

The voice of his former drug counselor echoed in his head, the dull hollow *thunk* of a heavy fountain pen against a cork clipboard ringing out as he spoke. "Your uncle the mechanic who kept a cigarette behind his ear for years just to prove he didn't have to smoke again was making a point about willpower." The counsellor had leaned forward, twirled his ballpoint pen, which seemed a little top-heavy to perform the maneuver with grace. "But your willpower and your genes aren't the same thing."

And getting caught with a cigarette was only a crime in high-school, and even then it would have been a slap on the wrist. Blake was mostly invisible, a nondescript white guy in pressed slacks and starched shirt. But on the off-chance he did somehow catch a cop's attention and got patted down, and the cop found the bag, then Jenda and him pooling their money to get his one on-record crime expunged was out the window.

That bleary-eyed photo of him haunting the internet would get some company, another image of him looking rousted, stunned, humiliated by the glare of a blinding light, making his eyes shine as if he had been crying. And he probably would cry if they caught him again.

He turned left as he came to the block of the apartment where he lived with Jenda, told himself he would leave the bag at the place as soon as he found a hiding spot. It would have to be somewhere she wouldn't find it, definitely somewhere Soren wouldn't sneak up on it, give it a single wet-nosed tentative sniff and go into seizures. If he helped push her back toward dope again…If he killed her cat.

Blake didn't allow his mind to complete either thought. Jenda wouldn't find it, and neither would Soren. And after hiding it he wouldn't touch it, except perhaps occasionally to lift the loose wooden board beneath which it hid. Just to taunt it and remind it he still walked the Earth, free and breathing clean air and drinking in sunshine, while the bag of dope stayed beneath ground, entombed where it belonged.

He dug his keychain from his pocket, the silver keys rattling one against the other. And as he did so, he remembered when he had asked the dope boy for just a taste. *Just enough for a car key*, he'd said, or words to that effect.

None of the keys on his chain were to a car, though. He didn't have a car yet, and maybe he never would.

NINE

A luxury coupe idled in front of the apartment building. It was low slung, sleek and tapered like a torpedo. The gunmetal grey body shined in the dark, the red taillights glowing like coals. There were a few dope dealers around here with nice rides, but most of those were classic American steel monsters with vogue-spoke rims and chrome tailpipes, Impalas or Caddies.

Blake walked around the car, giving it as much berth as he would a spaceship that landed in the parking lot. He could sort of see the driver through the smoked tint windows, his coif close-cropped and a shade of grey that reminded Blake more of silver filigree than hair. The man sat ramrod straight, maybe out of habit, maybe because having a car like his in a crap neighborhood made him antsy.

"Hey, babe."

Blake looked up, saw Jenda coming toward him, balancing Soren's pet taxi as she moved toward the grey coupe.

"Hey." Blake wasn't shocked, or even surprised. Even worse he felt relieved, though he feared that if he didn't at least protest, it would hurt her feelings. Their relationship had been very much an *any port in a storm* affair of two ex-addicts linking up until things got better or worse. Things had gotten better for her and worse for him, and it made sense for them to part. The breakup required no more analysis than an icefloe cracking because of an early spring thaw.

"You need any help?" He pulled the rear door open, several of the car's bells and whistles dinging.

"Thank you." She set Soren onto the heated, ribbed contoured leather pads in the backseat. The man in front turned his head slightly to both acknowledge Blake's presence and to signal he would not stoop so low as to greet him.

Jenda closed the door on the cat, exhaled, almost panting. No doubt she was tuckered from moving her stuff, but she was also excited, happy to be starting this new chapter. "You're not mad at me?"

He shook his head. She grinned, gave him a quick platonic peck on the left cheek. "Thank you for being so cool." She briefly locked her arms behind his neck, let her hands drape there, and stared in his eyes as if they were at prom and the slow dance number had finally come on. "Dr. Drakulic is going to help me go to art school. I've got to take this chance. I don't want to stick needles in people's arms, even to help them." She shook her head, and a cut of her pixie bang spilled free from behind her ear, dangling over her greyish-blue eye. "And if I stay here, not following my dream, I'm going to go into my phlebotomy bag one night, take out that needle, and do something stupid."

"I understand." His legs hurt and he wanted to get upstairs. He felt guilt that his pains should be so prosaic, that nothing like love, not even lust, clouded his mind. He wanted food, some TV, the warmth of a bed. And he wanted to bat his little bag of heroin around for a while longer, as if it were a dead mouse. Show it who was boss. *Thank God*, he thought, *I don't love her*. Leaving dope is like leaving a lover. Lose a lover while pining for dope, and you're that much more likely to fall back into the ever-welcoming arms of Mama Heroin, away from all the lame realities of the day.

She paused once, rocking on her feet, antsy, he prayed, for something besides dope. "You gonna be okay?" Jenda's already moony eyes went wider. He had the strange feeling he sometimes got from her, that not only did she love to draw cartoons, but that she was one, born of some draughtman's enchanted pen.

"I'll be alright," he said, trying to conceal the relief. He thought of how startled he'd felt the times she'd cried without warning, catching him unaware and causing him to freeze in terror on his half of the bed.

Maybe he just wasn't man enough for her. Dr. Drakulic looked sophisticated. Perhaps when she felt the world going off its axis, she could add another clothespin to his phallus, treat the penis like a fulcrum upon which she could safely turn the world at a speed she could handle.

But he wouldn't kink shame.

She ran around to the other side of the car, opened the passenger door.

"I'll be looking for your stuff in the comic book stores!" he shouted.

She looked at him one last time, smiled with her anime-wide eyes. "He's going to help me work on your expungement!"

Blake waved, embarrassed that she had shared the details of his pathetic life with the good doctor. He pictured her talking with Dr. Drakulic about him, the doctor peering over his readers as he filled out some paperwork in his study while Jenda massaged his shoulders and told him about the string of loser boyfriends she'd had: the bass player who borrowed money from her, the-

He killed the thought. He had hurt enough for one day. It was bachelor time. But it was important not to let it get out of hand, fall into a hole where he crushed takeout carton after takeout carton of buffalo wings and then reached around looking for a napkin to wipe his hands, and settled on using a pair of Jenda's old purple lace panties. But he would at least watch a fight or two, sit on the edge of the bed and exorcise his demons by viewing two tattooed bald men drop elbows on each other's skulls until a crack sounded over the cheers of the bloodthirsty crowd.

Jenda had never liked mixed martial arts, especially the more vicious strikers. But Jenda, soft, sweet, slightly psychotic, was gone.

He trudged his way upstairs, feeling somehow like an overburdened pack mule despite the lightness of the brown leather haversack he lugged. He knew what it was, the source of this mysterious weight, when he finally reached the landing, stuck the key in the door, and turned the knob. It wasn't the weight of being alone anymore.

Being alone was great.

It was the weight of the dope, the little glassine envelope where the grains sat. The plastic bottle of yellow piss cleaner Mikey Seever gave him still lay in the satchel, seal unbroken. It was a get-out-of-jail free card, an instant absolution of sin he carried in his pocket. Hell, because he could use it multiple times it was more of a genie, ready to "yes, master" any request for at least a few toots over the next few days.

He entered the apartment and smelled the gritty, chalklike scent of kitty litter in the air, tickling his nose almost to the point of sneezing. Those same cilia that almost spasmed in a sneeze now called out for a sniff. His cells screamed. The weight of his body's need was so much stronger than the will that had dissolved, practically cooking off in the heat of his hunger.

Dope would be the woman that no flesh and blood woman could be. It would be all the dendritic nodes both on his brain and on the phone trees, a connection of "Yesses" to every question he asked, every call a sell. Better than a car, it would be a chariot to take him into the sky and away from reality and being a weak man in a world where that was unforgivable, where he was less than useless.

He pulled the package from his pocket, stroked its plastic worn so soft it was like silk freshly spun by a worm. And he knew he could either do this dope, or he could die.

*

She had taken the cat but left the litterbox. Blake briefly considered walking over to Soren's box, opening the little envelope he held in his hands, and sprinkling the dope into the bed of Fresh Step. It had been a couple days since she had emptied the box, and clumps of cat crap caked with friable litter granules stood out beneath the sandy surface usually combed smooth as a Japanese rock garden.

Blake walked over to the nightstand, turned on the lamp. The faux malachite base of the lamp glowed green, and a pool of light spilled from beneath the brown parchment of the lampshade. He tapped himself out a line, a furrow he tended as carefully as if it were gold dust.

He pulled his wallet out of his back pocket, extracted a twenty from the row of bills still flush and crisp from the ATM. He couldn't use a dollar bill. It had to be something bigger.

It didn't matter how big the denomination; it was all cotton-weight paper and neither the ghost of Abe Lincoln nor George Washington was likely to bridle at their likeness being put to such use. But it mattered to him.

He rolled the Andrew Jackson big face bill into a tight tube, felt something catch in his soul, some dim voice that should have been a shout but was more like a faint, windswept whisper. It said *Don't!* He sniffed, got the first pull of dope and moved his nose in line with the bill, taking it quickly to the head.

His brain, usually dulled by fluorescent light, had once again locked on the old frequency, in tune with the harmony of the spheres. His heart beat like a Buddhist gong, the thrum of current going through him making him feel like he could make music through the tips of his fingers without aid of piano or guitar.

It would end, but he had a solution to that. Do more. And if they asked him to piss at work…He walked over to his bag, opened the satchel, went inside. Then he unscrewed the top of the yellow drink and took a slug. It had a slight citrus taste with a minty back.

Blake screwed the cap back on, returned the drink to the bag. He tried out his legs, found them rubbery. He walked back through the front of the apartment, closing the door behind him, not able to care about the cat shit or Jenda being gone or his war with Gabriel Paz.

The high still buoyed him as he left the building and walked into the street. The sidewalk was like meringue under his shoes, the usual feel of something cold and hard now as gentle as everything else. He wasn't walking through a scruffy semi-suburban industrial wasteland of crumbling brick and rebar peeking through concrete anymore. Instead, he was on that clipper ship that Lou Reed sang about, where just by doing something ancient and Eastern and opium-derived he would time travel. He wasn't walking beneath the wan light of sodium vapor lamps, old cars drifting on the road aimed toward a highway. He was the head of one of those papier mâché dragons shuffling through Chinatown, ruby-red eyes and sun-yellow forked tongue sneaking out of its mouth and lolling from the centuries of magic and joy.

The same dope boy was on the block, though it had apparently gotten cold enough for him to switch to a butter soft leather Pelle-Pelle motorcycle jacket. Blake sensed the boy's nerves, the cords of his throat taut, eyes scanning so hard they looked like they were trying to break free from his head.

An hour ago he was a death dealer. Now he, like everyone else, was Blake's friend. But even through the cloud of dope Blake knew the happiness wouldn't last, the divine secret would not remain his, unless he got more dope.

The dope boy stowed a rising smile, swallowing it since it wouldn't do to gloat over snaring a return customer so quickly, especially one who had sworn off dope a short time ago.

Blake's eyes shone like glass marbles. He didn't hide his smile, or his hunger. He stamped his feet and wasn't sure if it was the cold or if it was the need for more. *More.* "Fifty this time."

They turned away from each other, as if both waiting for the same bus but with no desire to chitchat. Blake pulled out his wallet, extracted two twenties and a ten, and began folding them as if trying to make a paper plane. He let the money fall to the ground.

"Bet." The dope boy turned around, his laconic bop masking the path of the baggie as it bounced beneath the fabric of his sweatpants and spilled out and fell through the striped raglan cuff. It got stuck there, and he waddled a bit. He lifted his leg slightly, adjusted his crotch, and the bag fell out.

Blake sniffed, bent, snatched up the bundle, not bothering to watch the dealer retrieve his money. He spun around, looked up the dark block toward the vanishing point where the lights of Midtown pulsed. He could feel the warmth of the lights as they glowed, looking on the pawnshops and strip clubs and cocktail lounges, their radiance as innocent as the baubles on a Christmas tree. Happiness lit him from the inside, but he could hear the timer ticking on the happiness. He had to move, suck what joy he could from the world before it settled back into its natural colors, the grey he couldn't endure.

He considered walking to a bridge, tossing himself off an overpass into oncoming traffic, and decided instead to do something perhaps even stupider.

Time-release lies, he told himself as he walked. That is what he'd been telling himself. When he said he would get the bag of dope just to show that he could hold it and have it without doing it, he had meant what he said, or rather what he thought. At least consciously. The rest of him— the part that was apparently calling the shots and making the feet move and saying *Hello* to him in his nightmares when he slept— that part had known all along that he got that bag to sniff it. The monster inside needed food. He worked for it, and as long as he did its bidding it would reward him, flood the brain with dopamine, keep a discotheque-like strobe pulsing in his frontal lobe. But if he betrayed the demon, didn't feed it the dope...

He didn't want to think about it. He had to keep feeding it. But it had other hungers. It needed something else almost as bad as it needed to escape the pain being imprisoned in him caused it. The dope demon needed to win and set the world to rights. Perhaps, he decided as he walked back to the phonebooth, it doesn't care for me, but it does at least pity me and wants me to find my small measure of solace. *It has to live with me, after all*

Here, then, was a small victory, to see the other man suffer the way the man had made him suffer, and how the man had smiled when he made Blake suffer! And laughed!

Blake pulled the floppy phonebook from the silver perforated shelf inside the booth, thumbed through until he found what he was looking for.

There was a little black-and-white graphic of twin wrenches crossed like halberds in a grease monkey's family crest. He picked up the receiver that smelled of vulcanized rubber, dropped in a quarter, and dialed.

It rang once, twice, three times. He feared no one would pick up, that the light he had found when looking toward Midtown was about to go out, that the voice he needed to hear wouldn't be there, as if this were a suicide hotline and he was getting nothing but busy tone.

"Yo, Sumter Bros, but we're closed. Call back in the morning during normal business hours, please."

At first he thought it was the most informal message in the history of answering machines, but the pneumatic whine of some drill or jack in the background and heavy breathing convinced him he was talking to a live person.

"Gabriel?"

"Who?" The person on the other end got no more out. He couldn't. His voice floated into the background as he turned away from the phone call with Blake. He said something indistinct. Blake couldn't be sure, but thought he had asked the other mechanics to kill the late night block of doowop some DJ spun.

"Mr. Paz, it seems we had some trouble—"

"Yo, you got to be shitting me."

"I shit you not," Blake said. "Listen, I think if I pull some strings and put a hold order on the credit hit, we can keep you clean with the Three Bureaus for the time being. I don't handle the structured payment plan end myself but—"

"How did you get this number, man?" The astonishment was still there, but it was washing away, en route to becoming something else. Blake could guess what, but he didn't care.

"One benefit of rebuilding good credit that I've found is that you can sometimes get waivers on hefty security deposits for things like utilities. It seems like a small thing, but—"

"Did you call my place when I wasn't home?"

Blake paused, wiped a coat of cold sweat from his forehead with the back of his hand, which felt like a sopping sponge when he drew his fingers back. He wiped the slick digits on his pant leg. "Just pay your bill, man. For me."

"What do you care?"

That stopped Blake. He leaned against the glass wall of the phone booth, breathed, and idly drew a shape with his finger in the foggy condensation. He wanted to answer, but it felt like a girl asking him to tell her he loved her. There was a reason he needed Gabriel to pay. He couldn't quite put it into words, but that didn't mean it wasn't real. Hell, the inability to put it into words made it realer. "Just pay…" Blake choked back a sob, and when he next spoke it startled him as much as Gabe. "Please."

"Yo, you crossed a line, violated. That shit is out of bounds. How would you like it if I come visit you at work?"

"Make sure to bring payment if you do. We need to settle this account."

"Oh, this shit is going to get settled, man. Best believe that."

"If you're ready to make payment now, I can patch you through to the collections bureau upstairs."

"Yo, my guy. I can *hear* cars honking and shit from your end. Do you think I'm stupid?"

"No."

"Yeah, good. You know what I think?"

"What?" Blake wanted to hang up the phone, somehow felt in the crossed signals of his brain that Gabe had called him.

"I think you're fucking crazy, bro."

"Maybe…" Blake shrugged, which shifted the warmth through the opiate-assuaged tissue of his shoulders. He shivered a bit from the rush.

"I'm crazy, too. You want to find out who's crazier?"

"If you want to kill me," Blake said, "you're going to have to get in line behind me."

"I got you, my guy."

He could see Gabriel in his mind's eye, no longer smiling, or laughing, but nodding to himself, making a solemn vow.

"You want out of this life shit. I dig. You're suicidal. I'm gonna give that ass a little assist."

There was a loud smack from Gabe's end and then dial tone filled Blake's ear. He smiled. He would take being a threat over being a joke. If someone wanted to kill you, it meant you mattered. It meant you had succeeded at something, if only getting under the other guy's skin.

And if Gabriel killed him? It would probably be a bullet. And a bullet was much quicker than the needle, which, he realized as he left the phone booth, had never really left his arm.

Save me. He blinked back tears, broadcasting the message crosstown to whatever shuttered shop Gabriel worked in, where he spent nights shimmying beneath undercarriages of cars on a mechanic's creeper, studying the parts he'd memorized in diagrams while in solitary confinement, the schematics having distracted him from screams and stabbings and suicides and dope shooting.

Shoot me, Blake begged, hoping his friend was telepathic and could hear his plea across the expanding bowl of the black night sky.

TEN

The good thing about having a mental breakdown was that most other people were usually cracking, too. And unless you were at a critical point—throwing file folders into the air, walking out onto the ledge of some building, pouring gasoline over yourself in front of the courthouse—no one was likely to notice.

And they were in the conference room, where it was dark, except for the light that speared from the slide carousel Bill ran.

He stood in front of them, to the side of the canvas screen upon which there was a stock photo of a smiling black man with a close-cropped afro fielding a call. Bill's blue dress shirt was especially loose, probably something from before his lap band surgery. It clashed in color and size with his black polyester pants that had shrunk after being washed on the wrong cycle. The effect was to make it look like Management had assembled him from the corpses of two previous supervisors, one fat and the other thin.

He pointed at the cheesing telemarketer on the slideshow. "So no, they cannot see you smiling.

Neither can the person on the other end see you sitting up straight in your seat while you're selling them. But they can *hear* what you look like. Not only that." He hit the cycler, and the screen went blank, the canvas white. "They can hear what you *feel* like. So if you don't feel like a winner…" His eyes drifted over them, and though Blake couldn't be sure, he thought Bill's eyes lingered on him. "Fake it til you make it." He walked around the walnut table to the far wall, turned on the lights. One of the Fishbowlers stifled his yawn when the light came on. Bill shot him a scowl, and someone coughed from the oppressive and warm scents of perfume and cologne that mixed like a noxious cloud whenever they were all here.

Blake stood with the others, walking heel-to-toe behind a shaggy-headed new hire wearing an unwrinkled Oxford-blue dress shirt.

Donna was back at her cubicle before him. She watched him with eyes that only looked impassive. The early morning sun gave the room a yellowish cast, making her appear slightly jaundiced, the otherwise-invisible papulose dots on her cheeks stark and apparent. "You slipped, didn't you?"

He looked at her. Her new hairstyle was perfect, Fibonacci-like spirals wrapped tight to the sides of her head.

"Oh, Blake." She looked away, shook her head, swiveled out of view. "I'll be praying for you."

His body itched, as if someone had squirted a whole can of sprayable starch onto his skin. It was the old junky's hydrophobia, the aversion to water just one of the many joys of addiction he had forgotten. But it was too late now. Either he got back into treatment (and gave up this job), or he robbed to support the full-blown habit creeping up on him. And he would have to buy bottle after bottle of that yellow piss if he was going to stay one step ahead of whatever UA Bill might plan.

Blake spun his chair to look in the boss's office. The slats of the blinds over the window were undisturbed. Then he opened his folder, went down the line with the nib of his knockoff Montblanc rollerball pen. "Elle Bangnara, Star Studio Nail Salon…" He looked at the notes he had written when planning to call her a few days ago, before he started using again. It was his handwriting, but it might as well have been a communique from some other him in an alternate universe, a time-travelling Blake Seever who hadn't relapsed. "Current product is better for ageing customers, but more expensive. Ask her if customers old. If no, save money and have more affordable product."

He took a deep breath. That slideshow in Bill's office had not only been a waste of time; it had probably hurt him. He didn't need a reminder that how he looked or felt might affect how he sold. Rather, he needed someone to tell him the opposite. He prepared to dial, hand steady until he made the mistake of staring out the window, saw the dope boy walking with his head down, hood up.

The phone rang, and it was like an electric current pulsing through him. He jolted up so hard that his butt lifted off the seat of the swivel chair. When he came back down, there was a crunch and the seat had lowered a couple notches, grinding through its pressurized gears.

"Telesolutions, Blake Seever." He braced for Gabe to tell him he had him scoped out from a building across the street, that he watched him through the sights of his sniper rifle, and to give him one reason he shouldn't pull the trigger.

"Blake, honey?" His mother. Mom. The ever-patient, the one who always forgave, the usable, abusable mother who remained a bottomless fount of love no matter how much hate the world and especially her son gave her in return. He wanted to hug her. But more than that, he wanted to hop in a time machine, show up on the playground in the past where she played hopscotch in a red jumper and pigtails. He would approach the kindergarten version of her, crouch down and say, "In about thirty years you're going to meet a man named Nathan Seever. Run! He'll wreck your life. And the son you have with him will merely be salt in the wound."

"Honey, the insurance is all set for you, the credit card is good-to-go, but you didn't go back to Hope Ways yet. Why not?"

He shifted the receiver from between his left ear and shoulder to between his right ear and shoulder, as if delaying might give him the time and talent to make up a lie. He had never been a good liar, except when the dope took over and fed him lines. "I've been too busy, Mom. Trying to make my quota here." He picked up the book, absently flipped through the laminated pages. As if the gesture might lend the sham some credence, on the off-chance Bill was right, that his mother might buy it because he at least faked it.

There was only breathing on her end, the raspy hiss and croak of a lifelong smoker. He wished there were some device, like a Hoover vacuum cleaner, that could suck the scars out of her throat, the accumulated damage to the tissue, everything that should have been wet inside dried by time and smoke. At least she didn't have cancer.

"Blake?" Her voice quivered.

He bit the inside of his lip to keep his voice from quaking. "Mom…" She knew. Why lie. "You gotta let go. Like Dad."

"I can't." She broke, shuddered and spasmed, openly sobbed. Hopefully she wasn't out in public, at the grocery store or the beauty salon, because that wouldn't have stopped her. She rarely felt shame. And while that had embarrassed him in the past, all it did now was make him proud of her, and ashamed of his own former embarrassment over his mother for— what? Feeling, caring, not pretending. Loving. That was the worst part, the love. "You're my baby."

"You can't let me in the house if I come by. Not til I'm clean."

"There's nothing left to steal." She laughed as she cried now, which was worse, because it reminded him of the joy that once had been hers some time in the past. Hard to say exactly when, but definitely before he showed up, before Nathan Seever planted him in her womb.

Blake held the phone tighter, gripped it so close it felt soldered to his flesh. He thought of everything he had stolen from her, first the wedding band and then the silver and the limited edition collection of QVC porcelain dolls in their little gingham dresses. Then he saw Golden Pawn again, their signboard traced with neon bulbs. He remembered the thrill that coursed through him as he pulled up (in a car he'd eventually sold for dope), gravel crunching under the tires. He could see himself once again walking up to the front of the grimy shack where the pearl-bodied guitars hung in the window behind the webwork of metal scissor gate. He could see the dude behind the desk, the hulking pawnbroker in his Harley Davidson wife-beater that bulged from the weight of his potato sack gut, arms crisscrossed with faded blue jailhouse tattoos. The man was a turkey buzzard sans feathers, feeding on the pain of addicts hemorrhaging their parents' retirement nest eggs, commemorative plates, precious heirlooms, and electronics. They sold it all just to make the nightmare that was time cease to dilate. To shrink everything to a pinpoint of no pain or boredom, no more of the drudgery that hung like a pall over the whole neighborhood with its work-church-work rhythms that wouldn't let even dreams breathe. The pawnbroker was slime in a way that no one else was, except maybe the dealers. But whenever Blake came to him, the man might as well have been sporting angel wings and standing before golden gates behind which ever-white clouds massed, smiling as he checked the holy rolls once before saying, "Come on in."

"Ma, I gotta go." Blake hung up.

Donna's voice came from his left. "That hurt *me*," she said. "Mercy." He could hear her blowing her nose.

*

During break he snuck across the street to Hope Ways but made sure to hoof it down to Piss Park before looking to cop. He went to the north end of the park, near the massive boulder where a cherry tree stood with its buds frozen shut and its branches empty. The kid in Gore-Tex desert camo stood still enough to give one of those human statue buskers a run for his money. Blake passed him and the dealer spoke as if automated. "Red tops, happy hour."

"Chiva," Blake mumbled, and wandered over the splintering wooden footbridge above the frozen pond. He came to the other end of the park where a copper statue stood, the city father surrounded by pigeons with dirty coats. The guy he already thought of as his regular dealer stood beneath a gaslight tricked by the overcast sky into glowing during the day. The dude kept his hands in the slash pockets of his Triple Goose down jacket. His hood was up, lined with something like fake chinchilla.

"You hiring?" Blake asked.

The dealer made his lip-smacking sound, clucked his tongue. "You bring me customers, we'll talk finder's fee."

Blake had meant it as a joke, but apparently the dope game did not engender levity. He tried to guess what the guy did in his free time for fun; maybe watched pit-bulls lock their jaws around each other's throats in basements.

They did the dance, with the dealer's half of the ritual nearer to literal, as he shimmied against the lamppost scratching his back on the metal standard like a bear against a tree. "After this, man, it's gonna be cut with that China shit. Don't need no bodies making my spot hot."

"I know my tolerance." Blake bent down to pick up the balloon wrapped in a shredded layer of plastic grocery bag. "If I die, I'll try to do it somewhere else."

"See that you do."

The dealer was lucky. Heroin sold itself, unlike green vending products or women's body lotion.

Blake did a beeline out of the park, cutting through the ice-encrusted grass piebald with patches of dead and yellow turf, until he came back to the main road. Others on lunch break walked toward him, lawyers in trench coats and leather gloves, cubicle jockeys like him wearing last year's winter jackets. He ducked into Subway. It was crowded enough that he could go to the bathroom with none of the sandwich artists behind the plastic guard hassling him.

The bathroom was warmer than the restaurant proper, though some of that warmth felt suspicious, fetid and humid. Reeking of piss. He pulled open the door of the first stall, its walls scrimshawed with graffiti, a couple artistic block letter tags done in sharpie along with some deeper-carved little devil glyphs and the requisite swastikas and racial slurs.

He opened the bundle, reading a bit of the red lettering on the plastic that shrouded the balloon, recognizing the name of the grocery store because he had bagged there as a young buck. Wherever the dealers bundled their work must have been some distance from here. This neighborhood was a "food desert," as Jenda had described it, nothing but chain restaurants with out-of-date Health Grades in their windows and convenience stores with shelves half-filled with ultra-high sodium canned goods.

Jenda. He wished her well, and not in the absent and slightly spiteful way one sometimes said that to convince themselves they weren't jealous. Any time a former addict really broke free, it was a victory for them all, a win over the Fates. If she had her first exhibit and called it "Ice Sculptures of my Loser Ex-Boyfriends," he would attend opening night without malice and compare his chainsaw-chiseled likeness there beyond the velvet rope to what he saw in the mirror.

He rolled up a dollar and speared it into the powder.

The toot through the bill hit the nostril, kissed the septum, and seeped into the mucous membranes. *Maintenance dose*, he told himself, stopping short of doing a contemptuous kingpin-sized snort that would leave him staggering bleary-eyed. Sure, he could get away with that on the street, even crumple over od'd on a steam grate and be nothing but an obstacle to foot traffic.

But he couldn't go back to Telesolutions on the nod. He needed just enough to boost him through the rest of the day, limp off into the night, and score another couple bags. He could pull this off, at least for a few more nights. Then the ATM would be implacable, refusing to spit out anything but bad news about how he had overdrawn. Eventually he would descend to the next rung, tap on his mother's door like a vampire trying to sweet-talk its way across the threshold of a warm blood's house.

He no longer felt the fetid warmth of the bathroom, and when he went back through the front, he didn't feel the chilled AC of the restaurant. He walked, briefly caught the eye of the kid with pimples, blonde hair, and multiple piercings behind the counter. The kid glowered at him, his eyes deep in shadow behind his Subway visor. The look was clear. *Fucking junkie.*

And *this* was the worst part, he realized as he went outside. Not that he was a danger, someone who could break into your house or bust into your car (he never did that, could always rummage, forage for scrap metal, shoplift and beg to get enough to keep from sickness). The worst part was that he was a nuisance, a reminder of weakness that everyone could look on. A fat man would see him drooling with chin touching sternum, waking up every time the nod got too deep, and in Blake he would see himself making his third run to the chocolate fondue fountain at the buffet. A woman who got carpal tunnel pulling the metal lever on the slot machines would see him before a shuttered shopfront, legs folded like a yogi; and she would look at his cup overflowing with the panhandling earnings of the day, and among that pile of nickels and dimes would see her sick scrounging for change between couch cushions.

Evil was better than weak. At least the dope boys took risks, showed cunning in avoiding the cops. Hell, they showed extreme willpower or at least prudence in not touching the poison they dealt.

He walked through the glass doors on the first floor of the Telesolutions building, took the stairwell that smelled of fresh paint. He wanted to avoid sharing the elevator with someone, especially someone from his floor and having to hold his breath and avert his eyes as the claustrophobia built.

At least he had gotten back early, which meant that most of the chairs in the Fishbowl were empty and he would not have to run the gauntlet of incriminating stares. Heroin wasn't coke, so it didn't create the sort of background noise of whispers or the creep of paranoia that turned mailboxes into SWAT snipers or radio broadcasts into mind controlling waves. But in some ways that made it worse. Heroin didn't do vigilance. Like with alcohol, if he was fucking up now he wouldn't know until tomorrow.

He looked down at his feet, moving one before the other, careful not to drag to his step like a Hollywood mummy caught up in its own bandages. He returned to his seat, exhaled as he sat down, stared out the window.

The phone rang, and he didn't pick it up. It couldn't have been good news, so he would delay it. If he could delay facing that he was an addict again (streak of many sober months snapped in one night), he could delay answering the phone. Dope was helping him keep some distance between him and himself. Now if he could just get the rest of the world to cooperate and keep its distance from him, he would have it made, sort of. For a time.

"You want me to get that?" Donna had rolled her way out of the cubicle, pulling herself along the carpet by digging her stiletto heels into the fabric. She had a Tupperware container in front of her, a plastic fork speared into shreds of a watery-red broth that smelled like vinegar.

"Kimchi?" Blake asked.

"Want some?" She held out the fork to him.

There was nothing he wanted less, but he shook his head politely. She was the last person he wanted to alienate. In some strange way he didn't quite understand, she was all he had. It wasn't as if she were his sponsor, but she was his something. "No, thank you."

"Your phone." She speared some spicy cabbage into her mouth, chewed it politely in mincing bites, swallowed, then spoke. "If you don't get it soon, other people are going to look over here."

"You're right." He picked it up. "Warden here. What say you, Governor?"

"Blake Seever?"

Some kind of eminence grise, the voice of a distinguished man, academic, dry. He could have been calling to give Blake results. A doc from Hope Ways wondering why he hadn't been in, sensing the worst? A lawyer maybe, if Jenda had made good on her promise to get something moving on his expungement? He waited until he realized the other man was waiting, too, whoever the hell he was.

"Yes, this is Blake Seever." Had Gabriel retained counsel? Nah, that wasn't his style. He wasn't a snitch. Then again, jailhouse lawyers could be masters at lawfare and he might angle to settle on a massive suit. Blake knew from orientation with Bill (and many warnings after that) that this was a one-party consent state, meaning someone could tape your conversation without telling you and it could be admissible in court.

The Gabe in his head was no longer enraged. It was back to smiling, on the verge of laughing. The fucker had won, had him beat.

"This is Paul. I came by to pick up Jenda the other night."

Blake waited, squinted through the pleasant fog he could feel evaporating even as it caressed him. "Right, the doctor."

"The da..." The man gulped. "The doctor." That had thrown him. Perhaps he suspected that if Blake knew his profession, then he knew his peccadillos. Blake had a thought, killed it. He needed money, but would rather go back to dumpster diving than blackmail some poor guy for his fetish. Nothing was more serious to someone than their own weird sexual thing, and that it was merely funny to everyone else made the mocking of that kink a cruelty. So the man pinned clothespins on his penis; it was a harmless pastime compared to putting needles in one's arm.

"Jenda went back today to get the rest of her things."

"Yeah, she left Soren's litterbox," Blake said.

"She told me that afterwards someone followed her back to my house."

Blake snapped awake, his high blown. "Did she say who..."

"No, she didn't say who." The doctor's voice grew dryer, acid, as if he regretted being sent on this errand. "I asked her if she thought you might be stalking her, but she said you were a gentle soul, mostly. Harmless."

His heart stirred at *gentle* and his bowels shifted at *harmless*. Gentleness was noble. Harmless was weak, a joke, a...junkie.

Not a tortured artist junkie, either, bleeding on the canvas in his skylit loft. Or a self-destructive rock star trashing a hotel room by swinging his cherry axe around. Just a junkie. On Mom's husband's insurance plan junkie.

"Did she say what he looked like?"

Blake could feel the good doctor squirming, and though this was an inopportune time to think about the PowerPoint, he realized Bill had been right yet again. One just somehow *knows* what the person on the other end of the line feels; one can sometimes see them through the phone.

"Yes, she did." The doctor paused.

Blake knew why there was a catch in the man's voice. He was an upper-middle class white man being forced to say the suspect was Hispanic-looking, brown-skinned. How to communicate his race to Blake without coming off racist? What if Blake was one of those uncouth working-class whites who, at the mere mention of the "M" word, devolved into tangential screeds about the "Messicans" taking our jobs?

"Hispanic fellow," Blake said, figuring "fellow" might make it more genteel, less...whatever the doctor found unsavory about admitting he had eyes.

"Yes," the doctor said, relieved that Blake had said it for him. "Are you in trouble?" The man's voice had softened again, liquid and concerned.

Blake wondered what kind of doctor he was. He didn't sound cold enough to be in cosmetic surgery or something like that. Jenda wouldn't have been with him if he were one of those billboard-advertising silicon slingers. Pediatrician, perhaps. Then again, maybe he was a surgeon. There was that sleek midlife crisis coupe that had haunted Blake's dreams since the night he saw it shining in the lamplight in front of his building.

"I think I am in trouble," Blake said, "but once that guy knows Jenda's not with me anymore, he'll leave her alone."

"Good," the doctor said. "I'd like to leave the police out of this."

"Me, too." Blake nodded, reached down into his satchel, pulled out the bottle sloshing with yellow fluid. It was only half-full now. Maybe it was a little brazen drinking it here, but he'd already decided it looked like Gatorade from a distance. "Doctor, I have to go."

"Listen, just so we understand each other, I don't want us to have any hard feelings."

"None," Blake said. "The better man won." He hung up. Then he heard a moist belch from the Tupperware that Donna had at her desk, followed by a scent of a cabbage that made him cough and tickled his nostrils with its spices.

"Man up," she said. "It'll put hair on your chest."

"Girls these days go for the smooth swimmer's look."

"Not me. I like it kinkier than the gatefold on that one Isley Brothers album cover where Ron had his shirt off."

"I missed that one."

"Your loss," she said.

Blake spun around, turned to the right, toward Bill's office. Fingers held the slats pried open. Beady eyes stared at him across an even expanse of grey carpet bathed in ceaseless fluorescence.

*

It had taken the rest of the can of Febreze to get rid of the smell of Donna's lunch, but Blake's work area finally no longer reeked like a Kraken dredged from the seafloor. Other workers intermittently sniffed the air, and though their grumblings were mostly low and muttered, he heard "something like squid" and a gripe about how it smelled like an Asian wet market over on his side of the room.

Blake didn't mind. It gave him some cover. As long as everyone's noses were on Donna's lunch, their eyes weren't on him. Except for Bill's. The boss had continued to break his fingers through the slats every two or three minutes to peer out, watching Blake with those reanimated eyes.

The phone rang roughly two hours after lunch. Blake picked it up on the second ring. "Telesolutions, Blake Seever. Eucalady will bring you euphoria."

"What's good?"

"Gabe!" Blake smiled, lifted his legs off the floor, and spun like a kid playing rocketeer in his dad's swivel chair. "Could I send you a cedarwood and rose Holiday Horn basket? Thanksgiving is just around the corner."

"So I figured out how you found out where I worked."

"Mechanics make good money. Probably more than I do."

That earned a hoarse laugh. Gabe cleared his throat. "Yeah, you're probably right. You ain't about shit so I wouldn't be surprised if I could buy and sell your sorry ass."

"How about buying some Eucalady?"

"You think you're funny?"

"I'm just selling." Blake looked out the window. A light grey snow fell at a slant, flaked so thin it looked like the world outside the window was an old TV picking up a stray signal.

"I told you, you stepped over the line. Now you're fin to get stepped on."

"I thought maybe your daughter was in charge over there."

"Yo!" There was more awe than rage in his voice now, as if even he hadn't yet comprehended what he might do to Blake, but that once he did it, Blake would have a hard time believing it, too. "Fuck, man..." Gabriel's voice trailed off. "I really wanted to fly straight this time. But it looks like I'm fin to watch my daughter grow old in pictures. And I'm gonna meet my grandkids behind a glass wall."

"Why?" Blake said. "Let's just hang up." His heart beat in his chest like it was trying to break free, as if even it realized what his mouth and his brain had done and wanted no part of it.

"Line's crossed, man. You fucked with my blood. *Way* out of bounds. We gotta handle this. My word is my bond."

"Fine!" Blake's shout surprised him, as did how quickly his own fear got replaced by rage. He had no daughter to fight for, but he had a mother whose suffering he could no longer bear. Maybe Gabriel was facing down life as a habitual felon, but Blake was staring down the bevel of the needle. "Let's meet."

He knew the idea of him squaring up to someone like Gabriel was a joke. The guy would pound his ass into the pavement and rupture his spleen until it was foie gras. But that beat dying one trip at a time to the ATM.

"You bring your chief seconds. I'll bring mine," Blake said. He didn't know where that came from; maybe since Jenda had left and he'd been binge-watching fights to make up for lost time.

Gabe giggled at that, some of his rage and astonishment evaporating as he got into the spirit. "You a boxing fan?"

"UFC."

"Man, fuck all that noise. Roosters fight in cages, Holmes."

"Odelay, carnalito. Tienes miedo de mis manos de piedras?"

Gabe's laughter sounded like a tailpipe sputtering its last gasps. "Your grammar's alright, but your accent's for shit. And like all gabachos, you got that faggy lisp."

"Blame Señora Carla Bangs, two years' high-school Spanish," Blake said.

"How about we compromise? Since you like to see men go at it like cocks with spurs, and I like the sweet science."

"What do you suggest?" Blake asked.

"Pistolas."

Blake's heart dropped, but he waited to speak, lest Gabriel hear the terror in his voice. "Sounds good."

"Where, when?"

The questions were coming too fast. But getting these questions at any time would have been too fast, as, in essence, Gabriel was asking him if he would like to die. Blake did, but not like this. The fear bounced around his gut like a child's rubber ball errantly tossed in a too-tight space. But when he looked out the window and saw Hope Ways, he remembered what his life was like and he could have hugged Gabriel.

"My mother used to say the only thing worse than doing something you don't want to do is dreading it."

"Yo, make sure to tell me where your moms lives before I plug you. I want to be the one to deliver the news."

Blake couldn't let himself get too worked up, because Gabe would enjoy his rage. Besides which, Blake had been the one to cross the line first, use the guy's daughter to get to him.

"Underground Parking Garage next to the old bank on Montfort," Blake said. "Twenty paces."

"When?" His unwavering need to know threw Blake.

Blake swallowed the fear so quickly it left a lump in his throat, like a trapped burp. "Today, after work. Six PM."

"Good shit. My shift don't start til Midnight. So I'll smoke your ass, throw the burner and my clothes in the incinerator. And I figure I'll have a Crown Vic on jacks just about the time Forensics breaks out their kit to find out who plugged you."

"You sound confident you're going to win our little quick draw."

"I'll bet you don't even own a piece."

"Wrong," Blake said, lying.

"Alright," Gabe said. "Six PM. Garage next to the old bank on Montfort. Don't take a big bag to the head before we get down there, either. Just a little snort for the nerves."

Blake's gorge rose as if the demon dope itself took insult and might crawl out through his screaming throat to tear the cholo apart for his little *chiste.* "And you make sure there are no INS agents around. You never took care of your status issues back when you were still picking strawberries in Oxnard before you got your first felony rap for stealing shiny hubcaps."

Gabe laughed through gritted teeth. It sounded like he was snarling, which maybe he was.

"Til six," Gabe said, and hung up.

A noise came from Blake's right.

"Blake? Can I see you for a minute?"

He looked toward the voice. It belonged to Bill.

*

Bill pressed his fingers deep into the surface of his desk, as if he were a sprinter getting ready to break across the blocks. His purple Dacron tie dangled, the triangular point touching the wood of the desk. He looked at Blake, lightless eyes swimming in vitreous fluid. Blake waited for him to speak, but Bill turned behind him to the row of grey metal filing cabinets stacked from the floor near to the ceiling.

If Bill were going to fire him, he would only quote Blake his numbers. If the cops were going to get involved, he might read notes left by some dick who'd gone undercover as a telemarketer to bust him. Maybe Mikey was a mole and had only gotten "busted" as part of his cover so he could debrief. Except Blake hadn't really gotten dirty by that point. His descent had begun *after* that weasel face got popped.

Who did that leave? Donna? He couldn't countenance it. If she had betrayed him, then the world was bereft of mercy. If she had sold him out, then it might be time to wait at the bus stop, stand as if queuing only to throw himself before the heavy monster before it reached the curb. He hadn't done the math but figured he was thinking about suicide every thirty seconds or so.

Bill went into the bottom drawer, which he had never done before. Employee files lay alphabetized in the top three shelves. As he leaned over, his shirttail spilled free. The faded elastic band of his tighty-whiteys became visible, lower back hair rising in curly, nearly pubic patches above that. He turned around holding a manila file folder in his hands, tossed that onto the desk.

"Open it," he said, and sat down in his chair. "Sit." Bill pointed toward the smaller of the two chairs, reached his hands behind his back and struggled to tuck in his shirttail.

Blake obeyed, sat down in the stiff chair that creaked as it received him. Then he flipped open the file folder. Bill dug around in his desk while Blake leafed through the pages. The topmost piece of paper was a loose-leaf bit of newsprint, as fragile as the outer skin of an onion, black and grey pieces of the copy flaking off like fish scales as Blake handled it. There was a captioned photo of a hard charger, something about the hawklike set of the eyes making him look especially virile. The man radiated confidence. Blake looked closer, wondered what the point of this exercise was. He read the inches of print set beneath the photo, realized who it was as he read. "JUNIOR TOASTMASTERS HEAD COACH CHARGED IN SEXUAL ASSAULT ON MINOR."

"Bill," Blake said.

"Look at the other one." Bill urged Blake on with a wave, then opened a jade-colored glass bottle of Cutty Sark he'd pulled from his desk while Blake had been reading. The boss guzzled while his employee perused.

Blake flipped to the next piece of paper, careful not to tear the fragile sheet he'd just been looking at.

There was no photo on the second piece of paper, and the paragraph of print wasn't much longer than a thumb. "The old cliché," Bill said, screwing the top back on his whiskey and hissing as a fusel-stench burp seared through his chest and out his mouth on a long exhale. "The bullshit story's splashed across page one, the retraction is on seventeen-b or something, a couple pages before the coupon section." He shook his head.

Blake closed the folder. He had questions, the main one being, *Why are you showing me this*? But this seemed like Bill's moment, not his. Typically other people were the last thing Blake thought about once the demon dope had him on tenterhooks again, which meant Bill's problems were big.

"It was sort of like the McMartin thing, a little before your time."

Blake didn't know what that was, so figured Bill was right. "This kid's mom sat around with her box of Zinfandel all day, reading True Crime paperbacks and watching Lifetime, and she somehow got it into her head that I was a monster." He shrugged, his bladelike thin shoulders making him look like a bird of prey perched on its haunches. "Maybe she was hoping they'd make a Movie of the Week out of it and Susanne Lucci would play her."

Bill drifted off, somewhere else, probably into the stratospheric heights of that corner office in the high-rise suite where he saw himself sitting now in some alternate timeline. He probably pictured it down to the finest details, maybe a gold-gilded telescope pointed out the window giving view onto the chopping grey waters of the riverfront. If the light and angle were just right, he probably could have spied the pitcher's mound in the new stadium from his office during home games.

Bill came back to himself, said, "I've been watching you for a while, noticed something eating you." He jerked his thumb toward the filing cabinets behind him. "Noticed your numbers nosediving."

Blake nodded, closed his hands one around the other to keep the fingers from trembling.

"And yes, I've been patching through incognito to see how you're doing with sales." His hand reached out toward his landline phone where it sat on the desk, ivory-white and fat-handled receiver nestled in the cradle. He stroked the phone as if he were a supervillain, and it was his direct line to the death ray that would lay waste to humanity if his demands weren't met. "I think I can help you."

"Help?" Blake wondered if he knew about his relapse. He'd figured they would have just bounced him on his ass if they knew. But maybe because people lateraled to Telesolutions from the treatment center, they had some kind of insurance scheme to help employees who slipped.

Bill dug deeper into the desk, and Blake sat there wondering what the hell would come out next. Depositions from the trumped-up charges against Bill related to the chomo case? Another green glass bottle of whiskey? If Bill asked Blake to partake, he'd have to decline. Drink had never been his thing, especially not while riding the horse.

Bill set a small metal object on the varnished wood of his desktop. It was a revolver, blued with a greyish molded rubber grip and a short nose. Blake couldn't be sure but thought it might be police issue. "Everybody's got their breaking point. I reached mine a long time ago." Bill pointed to the window over which the blinds were drawn. "I know what they say about me out there. 'Bill's going to go postal.' 'Bill's afraid the cops are gonna find all the bodies hidden in the drywall at his apartment.'"

"Nobody says that, Bill."

"I don't care." He waved it off with a limp and dismissive toss of the hand. His brow creased, furrowed so much it looked like his head was hewn from wood scalloped by a whittler. "But it looks like you've reached that point, too." He looked up at Blake, eyes wide, questioning, filled with light and reflecting genuine interest perhaps for the first time in decades.

Blake realized what the man conveyed with his look. Some inquisitiveness, to see if Blake was really ready to do it, pull the trigger, but also a barely concealed joy. Bill had been staring into the abyss for quite some time, but he had held back solely and strangely enough because he didn't want to jump into the blackness alone. He looked at Blake, hoping, perhaps even praying, that he was ready to jump, too. Blake picked up the gun, giving Bill his answer.

Bill smiled, clapped his hands together and then sanded his palms one against the other as if to generate warmth while fireside. He always got like this when he talked specs, brass tacks, though the gun seemed to give him a bigger charge than either the Green Vending deal or the Eucalady contract. "That gun's built to minimize recoil. A Charter Arms forty-four. Cops used to have them, but now I think they've got other guns."

Blake hefted it, the weight stable, seductive in his palm. He ran his fingers along the checks and crosshatching in the rubber grip, let his touch stray to the chilly nickeled grooves of the revolver's cylinder. He felt the first stirrings of an erection, despite what dope usually did to his dick.

"You know," Bill said, "speaking purely from a salesmanship perspective, you took the wrong tact with this guy."

"What do you mean?" Blake kept the gun in his right hand, finger just outside the trigger well. He understood the appeal of the thing, its power. Five minutes ago he had felt like a rat in some scientist's maze slowly being parceled little chunks of dope dissolved in his water feeder followed by intermittent zaps from some shock device. Now he felt like an outlaw who sat with his spurs dug into the wood of a table in a saloon taking potshots at the wanted posters with his picture on them. Power.

"You wanted something from him at first, right?" Bill asked. His eyebrow arched. He studied Blake with his right eye as if it were the only one in his head, and he valued it twice as much for that reason.

"I wanted him to pay."

"Right, so he strung you along, kept you on ice with his fuzzy commitments. 'Check's in the mail' or 'I meant to send it out yesterday.'"

Blake nodded.

"But after you pissed him off, he wanted to meet you, *needed* to."

Bill paused, waited for it to sink in, gazing on Blake with that unblinking eye.

"Shit," Blake said. "I could have strung him along."

"Still can."

"How?" Blake asked.

Bill sat back in his chair, gave Blake the two-eyed gaze now that he'd imparted the lesson. "Easy. You just don't show up in that garage tonight." He laughed, drummed his fingers on the tabletop. "You think he's pissed now!" Bill ceased drumming, closed both of his fists. He kept his hands held high in a comically belligerent pose, like the Fighting Irish mascot with dukes up and chin tucked. "Play psychological warfare."

Blake briefly considered it, let his pointer finger drift into the trigger well, held the gun up to the light. The fluorescence that did so much damage to their skin bounced harmlessly off the blued cobalt. Guns were so much stronger than people. "No." Blake shook his head. "We have to handle this tonight."

Bill dropped his fists, reached his hand out to Blake.

Blake stared at him, confused, thinking perhaps Bill wanted to shake his hand, to congratulate him on taking up the challenge thrown down by the debtor who had insulted his honor over the phone. Only after Bill's eyes darted toward Blake's right hand did Blake realize what Bill was asking. He wanted the gun back. Blake paused, the way anyone with a gun in hand does when someone else asks for it. The shift of power, the absence where there had been weight somehow hard to bear.

"Here you go." Blake gave him back his gun.

The grin still hadn't left Bill's face, and the return of the gun to his palm only widened it. "It is my honor to be your chief second." He picked up his bottle of whiskey with the hand not holding the gun, set it back in the drawer and retrieved a travel-sized bottle of green mint mouthwash from inside the desk. He stuffed the piece in the back of his pants, reaching around to where the shirttail had come free of his khakis earlier.

"I'll get there a little early, to scout things out and..." Bill's tongue darted out of his mouth. "Get a couple Bavarian crème crullers from Dunkin and a nice hot cup of black coffee." He winked. "You picked the right location for this little matter to get settled."

Sweat dripped from Blake's scalp, itching so badly he thought for a moment he had head lice. His eyes were sore as if he had been staring at a computer monitor up close for hours, and the insides of his nostrils burned like he had been snorting straight Saharan sand rather than fluffy powdered dope.

He had to get right before he met Bill at Dunkin, en route to the big dance with Gabriel. But he didn't want to overdo it, get so high he couldn't shoot straight. That would only amuse Gabe, and being a joke was the one thing Blake could no longer abide. Being dead didn't seem so bad. Dead was doable.

Then again if he was too high to shoot straight, he might also be too high to feel the bullet when it hit him.

Blake stood, thought about it, wondering if he might work in one or two sales calls before he clocked out at five and started on foot toward a destiny he could no longer delay.

ELEVEN

Like everyone else in recovery, Blake had read the Big Blue Book, learning from the life of Bill W. and trying to apply what he learned from the founder of Alcoholics Anonymous to the life of an IV drug user. The Bible had been there, too, not forced on anyone but strategically placed in break rooms, left beneath seats in group. It hadn't worked for him, but that might have been because his brain was fuzzy when he tried to read it, or the way the gluey scent of the book's binding turned his stomach. But he knew the basics and remembered the bits now as he walked. His mind latched onto the Twenty-Third Psalm, but he found he did not need its solace. He had expected this march to the underground parking garage to feel like his own personal trudge up the Appian Way, but when he checked his feelings and examined his thoughts, there was only relief.

Sure, getting his record expunged would have helped. But death was the ultimate expungement, a cleaning of the slate that would solve all life's problems. And who knew. Maybe there was an afterlife, or even better, reincarnation. And if in the next life he could hold some distant echo of the life he'd led here in the body of Blake Seever, then he might know to stay away from drugs next time.

He stopped in Peace Park, going directly to the north end because they sold rock on the other bit of frozen greensward. Acorns crunched open beneath his feet as he stepped off the brick path onto the patch of nearly frozen grass. His dealer was finishing up with a stocky older white woman dressed in a baggy hooded sweatshirt that went down well below the knees of her warmup leggings.

Blake looked off to the side, toward a pair of bare-branched lindens, watched a starling land, balance itself there and open its mouth as if preparatory to cawing. When he turned back, the girl had left, and the dealer was digging in his waistband. Blake wondered what might happen, if through a fluke, he got the drop on Gabriel and won their quick draw, and somehow the echoing report of the traded gunshots didn't draw the wrong sort of attention. Assuming he and Bill made it out of that garage, what then?

He fantasized, saw the bullet break through the Gabriel he'd fashioned in his mind, the ricochet of the pinging round chipping a bit of mortar from the concrete support column in the garage after it passed through the man. He could come back here after that, to Piss Park, stick up the dealer, go in his pockets, take his entire supply of dope, hole up in a motel and have some kind of Junky James Cagney spree. *Top of the World, Ma!* Or at least second-story balcony of the

Ramada Inn before some SWAT sniper picked him off while he waited for the hostage negotiator to make good on his promise to send in the pizza man.

Then again, maybe not.

He stepped to the dealer, studying his eyes in fear that he had divined some of his thoughts, knew about his plan to pull a stickup and take what was his.

"Alright, man." The dealer threw his voice, and it carried so lightly on the wind Blake wasn't sure it hadn't been in his head, or if he had mistaken birdsong for words.

"What?" Blake dug for the tightly folded knot of dope money.

"Like I said, this is that new ish. Hope you know that." The dealer nodded toward the hillock over which the woman with the sweatshirt and unseasonably thin spandex leggings just disappeared. "They been doing this shit for a while."

"More dope, less chat." Blake tossed his money, sailing it like a prison kite.

"I admire your sense of adventure." The dealer sniffled, laughed. No doubt he got cold standing outside in the park all day. Hopefully, his relief would be here soon. "Here." The shredded bundle of plastic grocery bag-covered balloon hit the frozen grass. Blake crunched more acorn shells open underfoot, wondering if that made them easier for squirrels to access. He groaned as he leaned over. The weird, nigh-arthritic and persistent aches that came with mild dope sickness had returned. The pains would remain unless he could stay high. And that was not happening unless he said goodbye to the last of his dignity, spent the nights here with the dealers and addicts, servicing hypocritical pastors and shamefaced dentists behind elderberry bushes or in a bathroom stall.

The idea of being a prostitute made him think of Jenda. It hurt, but not like thinking about his mother. That was true pain. But the bag would take care of that, too.

And Gabriel would do the rest.

Blake got back onto the path, his shoes scraping against the macadam as he walked. The last of daylight was fading from the sky, a patch of nacreous cloud lending a final touch of white. He thought about going to the park bathroom to toot, but the "toe-tappers" might already be in there and his presence might be misread. Because he was too young to be a John and still had enough of his good looks, they would assume he was there to make money. Blake told himself he would never do that. But he had screwed up enough in the last few days to know that if it were a time-release lie he told himself now, then he would only realize it after he went into that bathroom.

He killed the thought, remembered what Jenda had said about a shower not being enough to wash away some kinds of dirt. The dope in his hands was for the pains of the past and the present. If he were to start selling his mouth, his hand, his culo, then the dope would also be to take away some of the pain he picked up tomorrow.

No, thank you.

He sat on the nearest bench, opened the plastic bag, taking his chances that a desperate stickup kid or an addict might clock him on the back of the head with an empty beer bottle. The wooden slats beneath his butt were cold, the chill working through the seat of his pants and making him stomp his feet on the concrete. He braced himself on the curved wrought iron of the armrest, found that even colder.

Blue and red strobes whapped their way through the bare branches of the trees in the park, adding color to the bleached greyness that had held everything in its waning light until now. Sirens wailed. He wrapped his dope again, startled despite his sluggishness. He looked around, saw the dealer lift his arms so quickly that his hood slipped off, exposing pigtail-sized mini-braids. The dude cupped his mouth and shouted, "One Time!" His voice carried through the park, and he sprinted, leaped one of the boulders planted in a rock garden bordered with fieldstone slabs.

Blake stood, told his body to walk while everything in him screamed *RUN!* He slid the dope into his right pocket, kept his hand in there. *I'm just trying to keep my hands warm, officer. It's cold.*

He had two options. One was to walk out through the other end of the park. But if the cops had planned this sting, and it wasn't just the dealer's bad luck, then that meant it was a pincers and the crack slinger at the other end of the park was also getting knocked. Any foot traffic headed that way would get swept up, and was probably getting a good shakedown, which he couldn't afford without first hitting the bathroom to boof the balloon in a stall. And going in there to suffer the indignity of a balloon in the *culo* might lead to many other humiliations. And if he got caught, then? Christ, another mugshot, and this one for...*No*. He imagined his mother reading about it, her son some gay rent boy with his image splashed in the back pages of the local rag. He and Bill could swap scrapbooks, share war stories.

The other option, the better one, was to walk to the fence, grab onto a couple of those wrought-iron finials and vault that sucker. Once he was on the other side and safe, he could blend in with the cold commuters trying to get home to a warm meal and a soft bed.

Voices shouted behind him, but in the distance, not much louder than calls volleyed between players in a game of pickup football. He made for the fence, those usually menacing spikes looking like the holy points of enchanted spears. He gripped them, summoned up his old teenage lust for the chase, just like back when he carried a little gym bag filled with aerosol cans, ready to throw up his tag on an underpass or brick wall.

He hopped. His feet hit the concrete on the other side. *Freedom.* A rush carried him along. It would only last until his heartbeat went back to normal, but for now the adrenaline was doing what the dope usually did. He looked left, saw the path to the Dunkin' in the first beams of the risen moon.

Blake didn't bother to turn around to check behind him, instead putting one foot in front of the other. He would walk a straight line until he came to the donut shop. Then he'd reunite with Bill, toot the Chinese dope for courage. After that he would take his gun in hand and descend to the underground garage to finally give a face to the voice that had echoed through the dark corners of his mind these last few days.

*

Bill was already at Dunkin Donuts when Blake got there. Night had come and given a raw edge to the cold, and the chill numbed Blake's fingers so bad he worried he might not be able to hold a gun. And he hadn't even done the headful of heroin yet, since being interrupted in the park.

Bill watched him from the parking lot. He leaned against the hood of his maroon Mercury Grand Marquis he used as a makeshift table for the things he'd gotten from the donut shop. He scrutinized Blake with one eye, as if suspecting something. But the scrutiny ended in a wink. Bill smiled, his mood shifting as he stood aside to let Blake behold the spread on the car hood.

"Help yourself." Bill waved the twisted cinnamon donut in his hand toward the box of pastries.

"Don't think I can."

Bill nodded, bit off a segment of his sugar twist. "Nervous?"

Blake turned around, looked through the plate-glass window of the shop, checking to see if there was a bathroom. "Wouldn't you be?"

Bill finished his donut, wiped the cake crumbs and powdered sugar from his fingers onto his pants. He glanced at his sugar and cinnamon-dusted slacks. "I'm not worried about stains. Laundry day's tomorrow and it'll be the dry-cleaner's problem." He grinned. "I could serve in your stead."

Blake said nothing, thought about it.

"Think about it," Bill said, unaware that Blake was, and hard. "He doesn't know what you look like."

"He knows what I sound like." Blake shook his head. "Plus..." He trailed off. How to explain to Bill that this guy knew him better than anyone else, that if Bill stood in his stead Gabe would know it through the secret chord that attached them? "I need to do it."

Bill accepted that, looked once over both shoulders. "I gotta hit the head."

"They have one?"

"Provided you're not too proud to piss behind the dumpster."

Blake shot him a mock salute. "Go speedily to thy work, sir."

"Be right back." Bill walked off into the dark, a train whistle steaming away somewhere in the dark, counterpart to the pulse of sickly neon and eerie glow of traffic lights.

Blake looked over his shoulder four times in three seconds, waiting until Bill disappeared around back. Then he picked up the box of donuts, opened it, and placed his face close to a chocolate-glazed pastry covered in festive green and red Christmas sprinkles. He snorted. The dope hit his nostrils. Then the rush hit him. A new plateau of high struck as soon as the vacuum force of his sniff pulled the whitish-brown powder (whiter than usual) up through the rolled tube of the bill.

It swam in his brain and heart and everything stopped. Not just the pain, but the world, motion. The moon pinned to the corner of the sky envied him. His mother had not only forgiven him for stealing her silverware, but had absolved him of life and its burdens. She had reduced him to the size of one of the glass crack phials they sold in the park and placed him back in the fertile soil of her womb where he could grow again and start over, but do it right this time.

Bill came back from pissing, and Blake still held the box close to his face. He gazed into it, not so much like a hungry man as someone who'd breached Pandora's Box and was having second thoughts.

"Huh, I knew you'd get hungry."

Blake lowered the box, his arms obeying, but in slow-motion.

"You sure you're alright?" Bill eyed him skeptically.

Blake nodded, the air that usually smelled of diesel exhaust now pure in his open lungs.

"Let's move." Bill slapped him on the chest, a hearty love tap meant to fortify him and keep him from chickening out. He wouldn't have to worry about that. Blake needed to die on the off-chance that the last feeling one had in life was the one they took with them to the other side. All he wanted was to be high while sitting perched on a cloud with a golden harpsichord for the rest of eternity. Was that too much to ask?

Bill's voice came to him, but the words were from the other side of a tunnel whose depths were fathomless. It was like the paramedic's screaming when they hit you with the Naloxone, the *DON'T DIE ON ME!!!* coming as faintly as the chirp of a goldfinch on a high branch.

"...I didn't get blessed in most ways, but the metabolism is one thing I got going for me. I can eat three jelly donuts before going to sleep, wake up, belly up to the scale in the morning, and lo-and-behold, I've lost a pound. Drove the wife nuts."

Blake came back, returning on the wave of startled anger one feels when life yanks them from the brink of death and blows the high.

They had reached the bank next to the parking garage. The building was a giant Palladian-style throwback, faced in café au lait stone that revealed quartzite little pores in the rock this close.

Bill took the donuts from Blake. The box still had the rolled-up dollar bill in it, stuck in the empty bag of dope like an animal's snout probing to feed. Blake watched, unable to speak, unable to stop it, feeling through the cloud of bliss the beginnings of shame. With some distant chamber of his mind, he recalled the first time his mom caught him snorting. His eyes followed the line of the box as Bill lifted it up, and Blake's chest thumped to explode. He envisioned his heart swelling like a party balloon overfilled with Kool-Aid colored-water, ready to burst. *Bill could die just breathing near it.* That shit was supposed to be super-powerful. Hell, it felt like it was killing him right now, though it was some weird tangle of fear and joy, being loved to death by the dope.

Bill lifted the box, pitched the remaining donuts into the trashcan. "Alright." He studied Blake, forced him to square up. He checked Blake's tie and smoothed his collar, as if he were his father and this were Blake's first day at private school. "Let your aim be true. Gun's an extension of the hand. *Don't* put too much of your finger in the trigger well and make sure your trigger finger's not super-sweaty. If the gun falls out of your hand and hits the ground, it will cost you a turn."

"Yeah." Blake had heard snatches of what Bill said.

"Let's go."

They turned from the bank and headed toward the underground garage. Blake fell asleep while walking and woke up with the next step. He did the zombie shuffle until they turned right down a concrete corridor that echoed with the noise of feet clattering against the asphalt and the slamming of car doors. The day was already done for most office workers, but it sounded like a few stragglers were still shuffling toward their cars.

"Let's do it..." Bill's voice trailed off. He clapped his hands and they exited the tunnel coming out on the first floor underground. Blake felt like a football player breaching through the banner held by cheerleaders as his team jogged to emerge onto the gridiron. The dope moving through him provided the cheers, a cicada-like wave of unending applause. He let the joyful serenade wash over him and could do no wrong even if he tried.

A sound came from behind them, a click and a pop. They spun together, facing a woman who kneeled before an alligator-skinned attaché case with a golden hasp that had come undone, scattering documents onto the oil-stained and glass-speckled concrete.

"Shit." Blake rubbed his scalp, goofy smile plastered on his face, eyelids heavy as curtains weighted with lead sashes. "You need help, ma'am?"

His voice startled her, and she hunched like a panther on its haunches, the shoulders on her houndstooth blazer rising up. "Get back! I have mace!"

Blake held up his hands, took three steps back, almost tripped, sensed the heel of his shoe catch on the ground. The cement of the parking lot was smooth, but might as well have been the pocked surface of the moon. He felt himself falling backwards, but Bill caught him. He slept for the fraction of the second he was falling and woke when Bill gripped his spine.

"You okay?"

"Good."

He was going down a tunnel, saw Archie, his wise-eyed Golden Retriever he'd had as a kid, tongue of living velvet panting as he chased a tennis ball. Then he realized it wasn't a tunnel the dog was going down; it was the door Archie had passed through when the vet gave him the shot that ended the suffering in his ageing bones. Blake had never asked Donna if it was true about dogs and heaven, but he followed Archie through the white portal of light. Here there was no need of heroin, for something even more golden was the medium in which all beings swam, man and dog alike.

The lamb would lie down with the lion and dealer and addict would dance around the maypole together under the sun.

But then Bill was in front of him again. "You sure you're okay?"

"I'm good."

"Did they tell you which floor of the parking garage?"

A high-pitched whistle rang out through the cold air, startled them so that they turned, spinning away from the woman who thought they might be a pair of rapists or muggers.

The figure was roly-poly, wearing a mesh breathing throwback jersey in yellowjacket colors, either Pittsburgh Pirates silks or a Penguins shirt. "Rally one floor down!" He raised the pointer finger of his right hand, whirled it around like a pennant flag at the start of a race. The lifting of his arm showed lines of definition cording from his shoulder through his forearm, revealing him to be more beefy than fat, like a nose tackle in the off-season.

They walked toward him. The whistler, satisfied, started back down to the next lower level with them trailing.

"You think that's him?" Bill muttered.

"No," Blake said. "I know it's not."

*

They went down another level into the underground parking garage, moving in silence, their footfalls synchronized. It was weird, Blake thought, to feel himself moving higher into the clouds as he literally went lower.

"This them, Paolo?"

"This is them."

Blake and Bill walked over the cold concrete stained black in patches and smelling of motor oil. The dude in the jersey named Paolo walked over to a gunmetal-grey Volvo four-door. Gabriel stood in front of the car, squared up as if ready to draw. He wore blue twill mechanic's coveralls with an oval-shaped nametape machine-stitched above the right breast pocket, where something bulged, probably a pack of cigarettes.

He had his arms crossed over his chest, making the ropey thews of his muscle flex beneath the fabric of his suit. He stood back from his car, held a hand out to the chariot. "This the lowrider you were expecting?" Gabriel tilted his head to the side, clearly enjoying his show of restraint in car selection. If Blake had been sober (or in withdrawal) he might have smiled slyly because he'd gotten under the guy's skin by harping on his potential fruit-picking roots or barrio life. Now, however, and high, his smile was wide and guileless. It was a nice car and if Gabriel was happy, then he was happy for him.

Gabriel raised one of his thin eyebrows, causing the otherwise sun-smoothened flesh of his scalp to scrunch up beneath his bald, bullet-shaped head. "You have a little toot before you came here?" He mimed snorting, holding an invisible Bicycle card pincered between three fingers on his right hand.

The anger came back, surged through Blake, or tried to, as his body released a countervailing wave of poppied bliss through the blood. But he felt disgust through the fog of pleasure. Enjoying himself while high was one thing; having other people derive joy from it made him feel like a clown, the town drunk staggering on the cobbles for the amusement of the folk in the city square.

He felt Bill's eyes on him, boring into the side of his face and threatening to break his heart into a thousand shards if he so much as turned. How he didn't already know Blake was chasing the Chiva was any man's guess. Bill's mouth was open, eyes wide, betrayal written into the aged patchwork flesh of his face. Then he remembered the gun, pulled it out.

"Dirty Harry." Paolo laughed.

"Without the long nose," Bill said, holding the piece out to Blake.

"I decided to make it fair." Gabriel unzipped the front of his blue coveralls, went into his waistband where a glinting piece of alloyed steel glowed against his ribbed white wife-beater. "It's automatic. I might jam up, if you're lucky."

Paolo looked from his man to the two white guys some fifteen or twenty feet away. His smile was near-cherubic, a reddish Santa Claus glow to his cheeks even though his skin was brown. Blake looked at him, figured he was the baby of the crew, the one who got teased for eating more barbecue than everyone else at family reunions. Paolo stared at Blake. "You know you don't have to do this? Last chance."

Bill looked at Blake uneasily, perhaps hoping he would swallow pride, see through the stoned haze of his own stubbornness. Or maybe hoping he would go through with it. "We can avoid the bloodshed," Blake said, blinking hard to keep awake. "All he has to do is make a payment on his debt, or agree to structure a settlement."

Paolo shook his head, his face getting redder and his smile wide enough now that his porcine cheeks raised up and made his ears twitch. "Dude's a basket case."

"Basket case is about to get his ass put in a casket." Gabriel pulled the slide, chambering a round. He kept the gun at his side, his hand lined up with the creased seam of his suit. It was clear he wanted to lift the gun, but would wait for Blake to raise his first. For Blake to do that, though, he would have to get the revolver from Bill.

Bill held out the piece, rubberized grip facing Blake. "Remember what I told you."

Blake turned to Bill, moving on the traction-free bottoms of his shoes while staying in place, shifting instead of stepping, as if ice skating. He forced his spine ramrod straight so they could go through with the ritual, this changing of the guard in a bargain basement version of Buckingham Palace. Gabriel and Paolo laughed at Blake's little about face, and the rage rose in Blake again, the cloud of dope-induced pleasure no longer strong enough to take the edge off anymore.

Blake took the gun in hand, held it across his chest as if ready to take a solemn oath with a revolver instead of a Bible.

"Stances?" Bill asked.

"Let's do it." The smile left Paolo's face, and he and Bill locked eyes. It didn't matter that one man was a disgraced office manager and the other the chunky runt of his pack of gearhead cholos. The ritual gave them their roles, and they were footmen for their lieges, tending the honor of their respective masters in a battle for satisfaction.

"Raise 'em," Paolo said. He looked at the stopwatch on the wrist of his right arm. He glanced at its glow-in-the-dark face. As he did so, a third chin sprouted beneath his second one. "On three."

"On *my* count," Bill said. He glanced from Blake to the twosome by the Volvo. It was bad enough that his duelist was stoned to the gills, and that the other two had probably been in shootouts before. If he let them call all the shots, then who knew what could happen? They might have a signal worked out between them, some way to gain a fraction of a second by gaming a mechanism in the stopwatch. Besides which, he was a manager and he was good at being in charge, even if his area of responsibility had dwindled to a pool of pathetic telemarketers over the years.

Paolo licked his lips, cocked his head to the side. "Who says on your count?" He stopped looking at his watch, depressed a button, and the green iridescence bathing him and his patch of concrete disappeared. "You ain't even got a watch."

"I can count to three."

"Yo," Gabriel said, waving his gun as carelessly as if it were a flyswatter. "Who cares? Let the short eyes-looking dude count to three."

"Short eyes?" Bill squinted, looked to Blake to clarify. But Blake stayed locked in on Gabriel, the smiling face in his head now synchronized with the grinning man before him. He wanted to lift the piece, squeeze, even as he felt another hot wave roll over him, crash and pull him back toward sleep, toward death. The tide was dragging him back to the other side. He didn't have much time.

Paolo laughed, looked at Gabriel admiringly, like he was an open mic act killing it with his routine. Bill didn't like Paolo's smile any more than Blake liked Gabe's. Bill looked like he wanted to ask Blake one more time to tell him what the hell a short eyes was. But another glance at Blake let Bill know his shooter would not unlock his eyes from his opponent standing there in a pool of sickly light. Bill looked at Paolo. "What's a short eyes?"

"Chomo," Paolo said, oblivious to the way the mood changed when the word left his mouth, oblivious to his own role in orchestrating the change with one word, two-syllables that turned this from a duel to a gunfight. It finally hit Bill, and he took advantage of Blake's steadfast trance to snatch the gun from a hand so clammy with sweat that a drip fell from the lifelines of Blake's palm onto the concrete.

"Yo!" Gabe said, turning to Bill, his own gun still lowered at his side. "I wanted a fair one with your boy here. You're supposed to be seeing to it that we-"

The shots surprised Gabe, as battle-hardened as he already was. A fraction of a second after Bill squeezed, the left shoulder of Paolo's black and yellow silk jersey disappeared, the bone and muscle over the ball and socket joint ripped off as easily as a soldier's epaulettes.

"Ah!" The fat Mexican hit the ground and his moan tapered to a whimper.

Bill shifted his gun to Gabriel, who fired off two shots that thundered loud enough to deafen them all, his eyes wide as he squeezed. Blake stood frozen, the dream finally overtaking him, ferrying him toward a warm slumber he could no longer resist. As it carried him away, he wondered why he ever fought it.

Bill fell to his right as the shock from the slug breaking his floating ribs dropped him like a marionette with its strings cut. He tried to move his legs, but found that a ricocheting fragment of bullet or bone had severed some nerve cord or spinal column. His hand opened and closed spasmodically and the gun that had been in his grip clattered to the floor. He lay on his back and his other hand shot out to his side, making it look like he was trying to create one-winged snow angels on the cold concrete.

Blake fell at about the same time, Gabe's next shot hitting him in the collarbone, flinging him around. He felt nothing as he collided with Bill on the way down. They entwined on the concrete, tossed together in a pile like two lovers locked in post-coital embrace. Blake was still alive and felt nothing but a mild itch where the bullet hit him. He hadn't heard the screams from Paolo or the urgent pleas from Gabe as he dragged his bleeding friend into the Volvo's passenger seat.

None of that mattered, for Blake was no longer a man, no longer large enough to even sense his lack of significance. If anything, the nothing was something to celebrate, a liberation from pride and shame and everything else. He was but a seed, no larger than the shells jacketing the bullets sent his and Bill's way.

The last of the casings fired in the exchange made a pinging sound on the concrete where they rattled and then rolled beneath the treads of screeching tires as the Volvo pulled out.

Blake sat in a space small as a fishbowl, tight and vitreous, realized he was in some womblike, veined caul, sharing the pellucid pocket inside his mother's stomach with Archie, his Golden Retriever. He smiled, happy to be with his dog again.

ABOUT THE AUTHOR

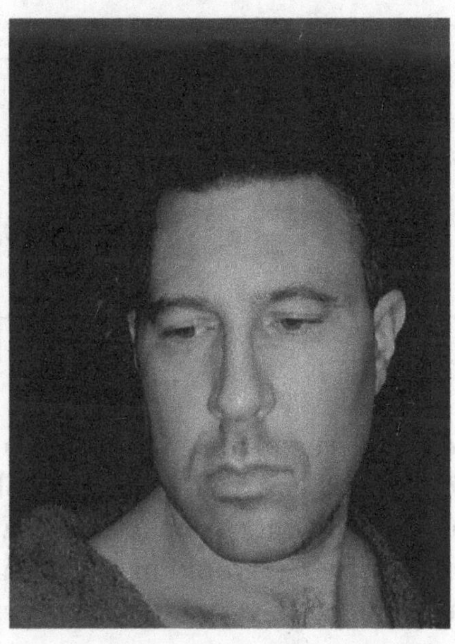

Joseph Hirsch is the author of several published novels. *The Phone in the Fishbowl* is his fourth with Black Rose Writing. His shorter works have appeared in numerous outlets, including *3 AM Magazine*, *Bull: Men's Fiction*, and *Zahir: A Journal of Speculative Fiction*. His poetry has also appeared in *Terror House* and *Retreats from Oblivion: The Journal of NoirCon*. He served four years in the U.S. Army, in which his travels took him to Iraq, Germany, and Texas. He holds an MA in Germanistik from the University of Cincinnati and is online at www.joeyhirsch.com. Lastly, he has a dog, a terrier named Tiffany.

NOTE FROM THE AUTHOR

Word-of-mouth is crucial for any author to succeed. If you enjoyed *The Phone in the Fishbowl*, please leave a review online—anywhere you are able. Even if it's just a sentence or two. It would make all the difference and would be very much appreciated.

Thanks!
Joseph Hirsch